SH

CW00504612

REDEMPTION OF THE HOPELESS

Sean Mallon Book Two

RICK WOOD

Blood Splatter Press

Rick Wood Publishing

Cover design by rickwoodswritersroom.com

With thanks to my street team for their help and contributions in both the creation and marketing of this book.

This book takes place two years after the events of *The Art of Murder*.

The End

Chapter One

A QUIVERING GASP PASSES HER LIPS.

She can't see a thing.

A piece of fabric rustles. She blinks her eyes with force, willing her vision to return. There's nothing. The fabric rustles once more.

It's a blindfold.

Her arms are restrained. Her ankles won't move. She is rendered completely and utterly immobile.

Her breath wheezes. She hyperventilates. She breathes anxiety, and she breathes fast.

A memory returns in a sudden punch, and an image illuminates her thoughts.

A Car. *Her* car. The door. Opening it. Getting in.

Something hitting the back of her head. Hard. Like wood or metal. She falls, and her consciousness ends.

Now she is here. But where is here? Moisture clings to the air with a fever that makes her throat close. She chokes on nothing.

She wonders how long she has left until she dies.

Shuffling. There's shuffling. Feet, she thinks. Dragging along a hard surface. A dusty surface.

She is not alone.

She listens carefully.

It's not feet. It's too constant. Like dragging. A body, maybe?

If it is a body, are they alive? They don't put up much of a fight. They could be drugged.

Was I drugged? she wonders.

Could that be how this happened?

"Hello?" she tries.

Shuffling. No response.

"Who's there?"

Whoever they are, they remain silent. She hears movement, but whoever it is does not want to talk to her.

"Please, let me go."

She's scared by the terror in her own voice. She sounds feeble. Desperate. She pulls on her restraints, but she is frantically bound. Blood surges adrenaline through the veins of her incarcerated body.

Mum.

She thinks about her mum.

A sweet face looking back at her. Smiling. Caring for her. So caring. So loving.

She'll be distraught if she dies.

She listens for a sign. Another clue to where she is. No birds sing, no light is cast upon her blindfold, no distant joyous children's scream from a park. Just an endless dripping of distant droplets of water. Her dry throat. A mixture of damp and distant smoke wiping the inside of her oesophagus with a scrape that makes her feel sick.

Something metal slides into something metal.

A hand presses against her face. It's clammy, and smells of onions. It grabs her blindfold in a fist and takes it off.

Her eyes open wide, but everything is blurry. She waits for her vision to adjust. As she does, she looks to every part of the room, willing her mind to recognise it. But she doesn't.

It's dark. The wall is brick, a single lamp shines at her side, a set of narrow wooden stairs ascend upward in the far corner.

Is this a basement?

Before her is a man. He, too, is bound, but only by his ankles. Whilst her entire body is restrained so nothing can move, his isn't; his hands are free.

He holds a gun.

Why does he hold a gun?

Why is he restrained too if he has a gun?

She knows him.

She knows this man.

His face. His green eyes. His stubble. The way his forehead crinkles when he frowns. The way his shoulders sit unnaturally high around his neck.

He has a gun.

His ankles are restrained.

Confusion mixes with fear.

He looks at the gun he nestles in his hands like a baby bird. He stares at it like it's the first time he's seen a gun in real life. Like he's in shock that he's holding it. Like he does not know why, but that he is starting to understand.

He looks at her. He meets her gaze.

He knows her.

There is a flicker of recognition in his eyes.

Why does he have a gun?

She remembers him. Finally, the illumination of understanding strikes her weary mind. It comforts her for a moment, then mortifies her, filling her with worrying clarity.

His name is Danny.

She met him a few months ago.

A one-night stand.

That's all it was, a one-night stand.

Except…

He had told her about something. Something he owned. A watch. That he wore, a prize possession, of great sentimental value – but of even greater financial cost.

His dead father gave him that watch.

That watch gave her £2000.

After she took it, leaving in the middle of the night, she didn't even glance at Danny asleep in his bed.

That watch gave her a whole weekend of partying.

"Danny…" she whispers.

He couldn't be the one who abducted her. He is shackled to the chair, he's also a prisoner. Except, it's different. Like he has some kind of power over her. Even though he's fixed to the chair, he's holding the gun. He is in charge.

He *is* in charge.

Of her. Of the situation. Just not his position.

He wasn't the one who put himself there, but he is the one that has the option to kill her.

As Danny looks from the gun to her, from the gun to her, and to the gun, and to her – he realises what's going to happen. She can see that in his face.

"I didn't mean to take it," she lies. "Please, Danny."

"My father gave me that watch. I told you how much it meant."

"I know, Danny, I know, but please, I–"

She stops talking. Bows her head.

There is nothing she could say.

To her, that watch was a quick fix. An easy sum of money. To him, it was heartache. Weeks of searching. Months of tears at the knowledge that some stupid slut stole it. She could never know what it was like to search endlessly, knowing he'd never find it.

She didn't leave him her number.

She didn't want to be tracked.

Yet there they are.

How are we here?

It is a pertinent question.

She looks around herself.

The answer presents itself in the form of a shadow. A silhouetted figure standing in the darkness behind the lamp's direction of light. The dark, hazy outline of a person, watching, ready, unknown.

The person steps forward.

Into the light.

Unlike Danny, she doesn't recognise this person. But she knows this is the perpetrator. The one who set up this twisted kind of justice. They have an air of arrogant belief. Of accomplishment. Smug at the success of their plan.

They take hold of Danny's wrist and lift the gun toward her head.

"You or her," the person whispers. "You decide."

Danny continues to look at the gun, then back to her.

He could use this gun on the person. He could end it all. Save them both.

But he doesn't.

Her whole body tenses. The skin on her arms prickles. Her heart punches her ribs.

"Five," speaks the looming dark figure.

"No, Danny, please, come on," she begs.

"Four."

Danny lifts the gun. Points it at her head.

"Three."

"Danny, I'm sorry, I am so sorry. You don't need to do this. There must be another way."

"Two."

She cries.

She pleads. Begs. Sobs.

Tears stream down her cheeks like bullets. Her crying grows louder, echoes against the walls, rebounding helplessly back at her.

Then she says the fatal words that seal her fate.

"Please, Danny – it was just a watch."

"One."

Danny shoots, and her body is limp.

Chapter Two

PERFECTLY ROASTED POTATOES, STEAMED PARSNIPS, FRESHLY cooked Yorkshire puddings; a mixture of heavenly scents trickle a tingle of elation through Sean's body. As Sheila places the roast chicken in the centre of the table, ready for him to carve, he can't help but smile. He casts his eyes over the luxurious feast, his mouth full of anticipatory saliva.

Mashed potatoes. Carrots. Stuffing. Sausages wrapped in bacon. Gravy. No one could ever cook such an aromatically pleasing meal as Sheila. He had intentionally eaten a small, unsatisfactory breakfast, readying himself for the forth-coming banquet – and he has not regretted his decision. His stomach rumbles, ready for the delicious delights he is about to consume.

Beside Sean sits Lily. His young daughter, staring lovingly at her doting father. Her smile shows Sean how thrilled she is to be sat next to him, how much she idolises him. Sean beams back at her, proud, full of uncompromising joy to be a dad to such a delightful young girl.

As Sheila places Sean's plate in front of him, she takes

hold of his eyes with hers, and places a deep, meaningful, longing kiss upon his lips.

"I love you," she tells him in a whisper.

"I love you, too."

Sean serves himself, starting with his favourite – pigs in blankets, then moving onto the Yorkshire puddings.

Once his plate is full, he lifts his head and looks at his family.

That's when he notices it.

He pauses.

Sheila's plate is empty.

Lily's plate is empty.

Neither of them serve themselves. They just stare. Stare at Sean, with robotic smiles.

He turns to Lily, stationary beside him. Still. Watching.

"Aren't you going to have any?" he asks.

She doesn't reply.

Just stares.

"Lily?"

Sean glances from Sheila to Lily, both of them mimicking each other's eerily rigid bodies.

"Lily?"

"Why did you hurt me, Daddy?" she asks, so nonchalantly it was as if she was asking him to pass the parsnips.

"What?" he gasps.

"Why did you hurt me?"

The words rack Sean's messy mind.

Why did he hurt her?

He would never hurt her. Never.

She looks down. Her legs. Bleeding. Pussing. Both of them torn apart. Dripping. Gushing. Inside out.

"My legs!" she cries, her stoic face now turned to uncontrollable weeps. "My legs!"

Sean does everything he can, but it's useless. He covers

the bleeding with his open palms. He urges words of comfort toward her. He tries to push the leg forward, as if he could fix it on more securely. But it's no good. It practically melts in his hands, and she does not stop weeping.

That's when his eyes spring open.

His family is gone. His roast dinner is gone. His happiness is gone.

None of it exists.

He is laid upon crusty bedsheets over a noisy mattress, the wires of which dig into his sore back. Sunlight glares through a gap in the blinds of his messy bedsit, stinging his eyes, piercing his retinas with an uncomfortable penetration.

A whiskey bottle rests between his drooping hand and the floor, dripping its sparse remnants over the stained carpet. He looks down and sees an open shirt falling off his shoulders, and a discarded pair of trousers still grasping one of his ankles. The right sleeve of his shirt is decorated in coffee stains and a pair of underwear beside his head pushes the drifting stench of stale piss toward him, allowing it to mix with the potent whiff of stale alcohol.

"Shit," he murmurs, shifting groggily, turning to his side.

There is a woman in the bed next to him.

He remembers her. He takes a moment to recollect her face, her pretty freckles and her perfect hair, and eventually he remembers that her name is Carmen. Carmen is petite and slim. Her perfect breasts rise up and down with her breathing. Her smooth, curved thighs entice him further.

He makes her feel both happy and sad.

Happy for her beauty.

Sad, as he wishes she could actually be his.

That he didn't have to pay for her love.

His head pounds. His brain attacks his skull with a constant throbbing. His mouth is parched, dry like the desert, his throat feeling like the scales of a snake.

He goes to stand, then falls back down, nauseous from the sudden movement. His belly jerks twice and he can already tell he's about to be sick.

He searches for something to catch his vomit in, firing his eyes around the room, scouring the dark spaces beneath discarded clothes and plates decorated with pizza crusts. He finds the brown paper bag his whiskey had been transported home in and shoves it to his mouth. His entire body convulses as he retches. A few mouthfuls of vomit spew between his cracked lips. The lumpiness of it makes him feel sicker.

As he looks down at the bagful of vomit he recoils at the sight. It's mostly blood. He is suddenly hungry but feels too sick to eat.

He discards the bag upon the floor.

He checks his watch.

8.40 a.m.

Do I have time for a shower?

He trudges to the bathroom, dragging his heavy legs across the crunchy carpet, unwillingly determined to brush his teeth. The harsh sting of the toothpaste grows painful against his sensitive gums, causing his ears to prick as he scrapes past various ulcers. The brushing makes his mouth bleed, so he stops and spits a mouthful of blood into the sink.

Collapsing against the wall, he groans.

Decides against a shower.

He'll just change his clothes instead.

Hope that no one gets close enough to smell the stink.

If they did, it would be their fault. There is no reason for anyone to ever get close to him.

"Hey," announces a sultry, soothing voice.

Sean looks up to see Carmen stood in the doorway to the bathroom. Elegant, sexy, bright like summer. She wears one of his shirts open over red laced underwear. Her long auburn hair floats over her shoulders and her smile makes him feel like a giddy schoolboy all over again.

"Hi," he grunts, diverting his gaze away. He doesn't want her to see him like this, though knows it would not make a difference. She wasn't in it for his looks.

"You look like hell," she observes, smiling cheekily.

He grins lecherously. "You don't."

"Are you going to work?" she asks. Even her voice is sensual. It sounds like silk gliding through warm fingers.

He closes his eyes and leans his head against the wall, wishing it would just collapse over him and end his suffering here and now.

"Building up to it."

"Could I have…" she trails off, feeling awkward.

He looks at her, confused, then suddenly remembers.

"Yeah, right, how could I forget," he mumbles, pushing himself up and stumbling to the bedroom. He opens the bedside draw, pulls out a wad of cash and hands it to Carmen.

She grins. She always looks happiest when taking the money.

He hates that.

He wished she looked this happy whilst she was fucking him.

"So, when are you going to give this all up and make an honest man out of me?" he muses, pretending that he's joking.

"I don't know – when are you going to give up drinking?" Carmen replies, pulling on her trousers and hoodie.

"I could give up drinking," he lies.

"I'll tell you what," she tells him playfully, placing a soft hand on the side of his face, sending tingles across his skin. "I'll pack it all in when you give up your search for Victor Crane."

13

He falls silent. Becomes numb with despair. But he doesn't let her see it. He drops his head, so she can't tell.

No woman ever sticks around.

Because they want to come first. And they never will.

Never.

Not even this Godly, beautiful whore. This touchable dream. This magnificent illusion of a perfect woman.

Not whilst the notorious psychopathic serial killer that paralysed his daughter is still out there, free to walk around.

"I'll see you, Sean." She kisses him on the cheek and leaves, knowing what the silence means.

He watches her go, staring at her swaying form side to side, her curves curving in all the right places.

He sighs. Runs his hands through his greasy hair. Pops two paracetamols, two ibuprofens, and leaves.

Dear Sean,

It has been a few weeks since I last wrote to you, so I wanted to send a brief correspondence, just to make sure that you are keeping well, and to let you know that I am, of course, thinking of you.

You would probably like to know where I am, or how I know your address. In fact, I can envisage you sending this letter for forensic analysis almost instantly upon your receiving it. Just know that it would be pointless. Inevitably, I imagine you would still try – but I am no fool, Sean. As you are well aware.

But there is no need to worry at the thought that I have acquired this information. I do not intend, under current circumstances, to come and murder you in your sleep. Not at the moment, anyway.

Though, if we are honest with each other, I imagine that you wouldn't mind that, would you?

If someone were to come put you out of your misery, you would likely thank them for the delightful service that they have provided to you.

I do worry about you, Sean.

Just imagine, for a fleeting moment, if the most unlikely of events happened, and you did catch me.

What then?

Your life would be void of purpose.

I worry that you would simply cease to exist. I am your biggest – no, let's be frank – your only reason to live. Without me, without this quest, what would you have left?

Disgraced by your daughter.

Deserted by your ex-wife.

Spending most of your nights with a prostitute that will never fully commit to you.

Your ex-wife even changed your daughter's name so you couldn't hurt her, yet you still ended up putting her in mortal danger simply by knowing her. She's hurt for life because of you, Sean, I hope you know that.

And that prostitute. She is the pick of the litter, Sean, I will give you that. But let her go. She will never give you what you dream of.

Do you dream, Sean?

I don't.

Yet if I did, I know I would dream of you. Of this friendship. Knowing how much we mean to each other. Knowing how one of us could not go on without the other. Knowing that, should one of us perish, the other would lose a piece of themselves. I hope that one day we could sit down in a coffee shop and discuss how much we actually mean to each other, but I know we are not at the point yet. I live in hope.

I do like to keep up with what's happening in your life, but know that I have no intention of interfering. I just like to watch. To know how helpless you are at catching me, as you will always be.

But please do clean yourself up, Sean.

You're a mess.

Have some dignity.

Please take care.

I do worry.

Yours in peaceful friendship,

Victor.

Chapter Three

SEAN WIPES HIS CLAMMY BROW ON THE BACK OF HIS WORN sleeve.

Alcohol sweats.

Again.

He rubs his neck. It perspires like he's in a deep summer's heat, yet he feels cold as winter. His forehead throbs rhythmically, a shaking bump pulsing in and out, in and out. He scratches his crotch, his dick aching from being thrust into Carmen with his typically animalistic aggression. The thought should be a good one, but it's still tormented by his wounded ego that aches in the knowledge that he must pay her to tolerate his company.

Sighing, he surveys the board as he does every day. It takes the whole width of the far wall of the incident room. And still, it does not get him any closer.

In the middle of the board is a CCTV picture of Victor Crane from a sighting eighteen months ago – the last confirmed sighting of Victor, strolling through an Aldi in Swindon, winking at the camera. Strings connect images of victims to various points of a map, accompanied by profiles and notes next to the faces of these poor ill-fated souls. Across the rest of the board is everything else they have, however little that may be. Forensic reports. Post-mortem examination notes. Near misses. Clues.

Every damn thing Sean had accumulated over the last two years of his vigorous endeavour to track down the bastard who paralysed his estranged daughter.

All of it is for nothing. He is no closer now than he has ever been. He'd had a few near misses that amounted to bugger all – just speculation mixed with hope mixed with desperation. He was about as close to finding Victor Crane as he was to being sober.

The investigation hadn't always been shrouded in pessimism. Two years ago, they managed to arrest Victor Crane's accomplice, Jack, who had disguised himself as Sean's apprentice. Sean had had to let Victor go in order to save his daughter's life. Having been so close, they were sure they were onto something – believing unequivocally that they were going to find Victor Crane right around the next figurative corner.

At that point, Sean's team had been twelve strong. Twelve officers dedicated to tracking down this psychopath. But, as weeks turned into months, more and more officers were needed for other cases that were deemed more 'solvable.' Lack of progress severely hindered the faith of Sean's superiors, and eventually he was left with his own company, and whichever young officer got dragged into this for 'experience.'

Experience.

"Hah," Sean grunts a sarcastic laugh at the thought.

Fuck experience.

Sean was experienced. He was once known as *the psychopath hunter* – the man who caught one of the country's most prolific serial killers. The man who independently took down the leader of a murderous paedophile ring. The press painted him as a hero, and other police officers spoke about him as a legend.

Then he killed the leader of that paedophile ring in cold blood rather than turn him in. He'd had no idea Sean's new apprentice had been a loyal part of that ring, and Sean let Jack con him into thinking they were friends. Whilst Sean was battling his post-traumatic stress disorder, Jack abducted Sean and his daughter with Victor's help, tied him to a chair, and began to stream his execution live over the internet.

Sean escaped, as did Victor, but only after Victor had taken Sean's daughter's ability to walk.

Now he's barely even a has-been. He's ignored. Ridiculed. Beside August Daniels, there is not a person in the station who has any remaining faith in the man he once was. None of them see through this fucked-up exterior – and he does not blame them for it. Because he knows that is all he is. All he has become.

He gets paid a pointless pay check that he blows on booze and whores in order to chase shadows of a man who screwed up his family and made them hate him.

Experience.

It isn't worth a damn thing.

August had often tried to tempt Sean away from the case. Get him to take a break. Have a look at something else, advise on another killer they were struggling on.

He just doesn't understand.

No one understands.

Victor Crane not only killed and raped several victims, some of which were children – he phoned Sean and told him about it, revealing Sean's secrets as a way to keep him quiet. Victor Crane systematically manipulated his partner against him, kidnapped his daughter, and left him as nothing but a wreckage of an existence that even rats in the sewers would decline.

Sean chose to save his daughter. But he never saw her again after that.

He couldn't do that to her.

He couldn't force her to have to deal with him in her life. Not just the danger she was in, but the pathetic sack-of-shit-father he was. She has a step-father now, who loves her – not as much as Sean does, he has no doubt about that – but a man that provides her with the warmth and comfort Sean could never give.

Sean is not being a coward, he assures himself of that. He is doing what's best for her.

He would always be a burden. A girl is better off growing up with the opportunities a real man could give her. She is better off without some loser-arsehole fucking up her life all the time. Being a part of her life is selfish, and he has to think of what is best for her.

Besides, this is his life now.

He looks at the clock.

Looks at the booze draw.

He should wait until midday. He should be resolved, disciplined.

But as the clock turns from 10.59 a.m. to 11.00 a.m., and he grows sick of another day sat there staring at this board, he decides it is late enough.

11.00 a.m. is the new midday.

He opens the desk draw, having to give it a yank as it gets jammed. He withdraws a bottle of whiskey, bypassing the dirty glass upon his cluttered desk and gulps a large swig straight from bottle. The sharp sting of the alcohol doesn't even phase him anymore. He drinks it down like it's orange juice.

He slumps down in his chair and tilts his head back,

finding it too heavy to hold up. It's a sunny day outside, but the curtains keep it out. Keep him in darkness.

He doesn't need to see the sun.

Or the blue sky.

Or the nearby park.

Nor does he need to hear the children laughing.

It will all end soon.

He rummages through his desk drawer, checking it's still there, just as he does every day. Ready for when he needs to use them.

They are still there.

Where they always are.

A bottle of pills confiscated from a drug addict and unknowingly misplaced. A half empty bottle of bleach, taken from a cupboard beneath the sink in the cleaner's office.

Ready.

Ready for when the time comes.

His reward for achieving his goal. For winning in an investigation that will never end.

Victor Crane is all he lives for now. It is all he cares about.

And once he captures him, that is it.

Done.

Over.

Finito.

No reason to go on.

He is ready to do what he must. To stop this pain. To dull the nagging anguish of incessant life.

To cease the voices in his head that bully him into submission. To kill the self-hatred, the self-loathing, the complete redundancy to his existence.

Living is futile.

He gazes upon the board once more. Runs his eyes back and forth, looking for something new, a clue, a new thought or hypothesis not yet entertained. Something that will illuminate his skilled detective ability with a stark realisation as to where Victor is. Something he has missed. Something obvious.

But all he sees is the same board he has looked at for the last two years. The only part of the room preserved in perfect condition.

Nothing sticks out.

Nothing ever does.

So he sits there.

Drinking.

Smoking.

Wondering when it is all going to end.

Wondering when he will finally catch Victor Crane.

And when he does, he has no intention of making an arrest.

A New Body

Chapter Four

IT'S TWELVE YEARS EARLIER AND AUGUST IS TWENTY-TWO years old. He takes care of his stamina and athleticism and has the natural energy of a man in his early twenties. Although if you were to accuse August of being young, you would be wrong; the head upon his shoulders is wiser than many of his older peers.

Even so, he lays awake in bed, staring up at the ceiling.

That day's events play through his mind like a bad movie.

His slip. His fall. Officers clattering to the ground around him. Then, worst of all, looking up to see the smug face of their suspect glancing back at the useless pile of police offi-cers. The suspect grins at them flailing over each other before taking the opportunity to escape.

It was his fault.

He is just a trainee. And he screwed-up. Never mind whether they pass his training or not, he was going to have to go into work the next day and look all these people in the eye, knowing how long they took to find this suspect. Knowing the effort and energy and restless nights and investigations and bodies and minds that it took just to secure a location.

His head turns to the alarm clock. It's gone three in the morning.

He knows he won't sleep. But he knows that he can't enter his morning shift without any rest. That could only cause more pathetic mishaps.

He could call in sick, but what then?

They'd all think it's because he can't face them.

His hand reaches out and ends up on his phone. Without even realising it, he's scrolled through his contacts, found Sean's number and placed the phone to his ear.

It rings numerous times, but his reliable friend answers without fail.

"August, you all right?" answers a meek voice.

"Sorry mate, did I wake you?" August asks, knowing full well that he did.

A sigh breathes through the phone – but not a frustrated or irritated one. Sean is too good for that. Just one that demonstrates his tired state.

"Yeah," Sean answers huskily. "Give me a sec'."

After a minute of shuffling and the squeak of a door, Sean's voice returns, just as weary but a little stronger.

"Okay man, what's up?" Sean says.

"Didn't wake Sheila as well, did I?"

"Nah, she's asleep."

"Good. I can't rest. It's just–"

"Today, right?" Sean always knows. "Yeah, it was a bad fuckup, I give you that."

Despite being such a blatant, harsh way of putting it, it is accompanied with a playful honesty that somehow gives August reassurance.

"That bad, huh?" August says.

"Mate, it was like you were the bowling ball and it was a lot of tenpin coppers."

August snorts a laugh.

"They went down better than your wife," Sean joked.

"Hey, don't be starting on her!"

"Well someone's got to."

They chuckle.

"Look," Sean says, "You messed up. And people are going to be pissed off tomorrow, I ain't going to lie to you. But it's not going to stop you passing."

"You think?"

"How many trainees have screwed-up before? I don't mean tripping over your feet like a fucking clown" – August laughs – "I mean, arresting the wrong guy, losing a witness statement, something that actually comes from being an idiot. How many people have done that, do you reckon?"

"Probably me in the next few weeks."

"No, it won't be, 'cause you're a good officer, and they ain't going to stop a good officer progressing just because he's been a bit of a knobhead. Are they?"

August huffs.

He's right.

Of course, he is.

"Thanks, mate," August says.

"Don't mention it."

"Why do you pick up your phone at gone three in the morning, though?" August teases. "What's that about?"

"I always answer my phone. Especially if it's you."

August smiles. He hears a baby crying from Sean's end of the line.

"Got to go," Sean announces.

"Yeah, cheers Sean."

He says his goodbyes and lets Sean go see to his daughter

– hoping that she doesn't wake Sheila. He doesn't want to be the one facing her wrath.

He drops his head back.

Tomorrow morning is going to be shit, but he just has to deal. He can face it. Take the flack, and in a few days, it'll be fine.

He closes his eyes and falls asleep.

Chapter Five

A HEAVY THROTTLE OF SEAN'S SHOULDER JERKS HIM AWAKE. His hazy eyes search the room, jolting into action as he grows abruptly alert.

He is in his office.

What time is it?

2.47 p.m. according to a nearby clock.

His whiskey bottle lies empty upon the floor next to a dribbling wet patch.

"Fuck..." he mutters.

That was good whiskey.

"Sean?" comes an urgent female voice from beside him.

"What?" he grunts bad-temperedly, his pounding headache returning with a vengeance. "What do you want?"

"Sean, you will definitely want to see this."

Detective Constable Elizabeth Hurks stands before him, excitedly prodding a set of photos in his belligerent face. He snatches them off her and awaits his vision's focus.

Elizabeth is an attractive young officer in her mid-twenties, with long black hair tied back and a slender figure. A pleasant woman, yet to be jaded by her years in the police.

Sean has always thought it's a shame that she's a police officer, as she has too much going for her. She's too pretty to be fighting drunks on a Saturday night. She shouldn't be the one fighting them – she should be the one they are fighting over.

Still, Sean knows he shouldn't think such things – nowadays, if you voice such an opinion, an army of female officers would be ready to hang you by your eyeballs. They were forced to attend a seminar about it, where the whole station was forced to sit for three hours and watch a group of ironically unattractive women assert that "you are only allowed to measure an officer's worth by their competency at their job."

Which means, as far as Sean is concerned, Elizabeth is bloody worthless.

He finds her to be inexperienced and frequently naïve. She had been part of the team that had originally helped track Victor Crane, and her contributions were always less than helpful. She has the ability to always see the positive in people.

Positive.

What fucking positive?

There is no positive.

People are scum. And if someone isn't scum, just wait long enough, and they will eventually be scum.

Sean doesn't see the world as she does.

He sees it for what it is.

The home of pointless existences prattling around until the joy of death finally releases them from their meaningless conflicts and arbitrary anxieties.

The pictures Elizabeth hands to Sean are of a tyre track. Nothing else.

"Why are you handing me this?" he demands in a hushed, aggravated tone, not caring about the hostility in his voice.

"Look at the next one."

Sean looks at the second image and grows instantly excited. It is the aerial view of an allotment, with a distinctly recognisable figure handling a bunch of flowers.

"Where did you get this?" Sean asks, feeling the blood rush through him.

"Found it in an orchard five days ago."

He holds the image of the tyre out in front of him again.

"And why have I got this?"

"We found this tyre track at a crime scene a week ago, where a young woman was robbed and assaulted. It has traces of the flowers Crane looks to have been handling."

Sean jumps from his seat.

Now we're talking!

He is already shaking. Whether it's alcohol or excitement, he isn't sure, but he feels light, giddy, like a schoolboy who just asked out his crush.

"Have you tracked it?"

"Yes." Elizabeth's grin spread from cheek to cheek. "We have him on CCTV of a café just out of town thirty minutes ago."

"And?" Sean demands, charging out of the room. Elizabeth scuttles behind him, trying to keep up.

"Officers have reached the café, and he's still there. They are awaiting your orders."

Sean's mind flutters through a dozen thoughts. How excited he is, how close they are, how he can't let this opportunity go, how he needs to hurry, and what he's going to do when he finally gets his hands on Victor Crane.

We have him. We actually have him.

And now he's finally going to kill him.

"You drive," Sean barks at Elizabeth. "How far?"

"Five minutes with flashing lights."

Sean picks his pace up into a run, barging his colleagues

out of the way, storming through the waiting room and toward the nearest car.

Elizabeth matches his speed. She gets into the driver's seat, hastily starts the car and skids away, sirens wailing, blue lights flashing, onto the road and through a set of red lights.

Sean sweats. A mixture of booze and elation.

Finally, he can put this to rest.

Finally, he can catch this prick and end everything.

They have him.

He feels like a kid at Christmas. Waiting to unwrap his present. Waiting to open it up and kill him.

Kill the fucker.

Do to him what he did to Sean.

So close now

So close.

Chapter Six

NUMEROUS CARS SWERVE OUT OF THE WAY OF THE FLASHING blue lights. Elizabeth overtakes them, swearing under her breath at any cars that take too long to move.

An old man panics behind the wheel of his Ford Focus and Elizabeth has to slam on the brakes. Sean curses him for being too old to drive, then tries to calm himself, reminding himself that he needs to be cool, he needs to be thinking straight and rationally. Victor Crane is smart, and this won't be as simple as it seems, and he needs to be at his best. He needs to separate himself from his emotions.

Until he gets his hands on Victor, that is – then his emotions will do all the talking.

He grabs the radio.

"This is Mallon, confirm you still have visual on target, over."

"Roger that, Detective," replies an obedient voice.

"Keep your distance. I repeat, do not move in until I get there. Tell me the second the target moves. Confirm instructions, over."

"Roger, Sean, we won't let him leave, over."

His leg bounces so hard he worries he may take off. His entire body surges with adrenaline, his mind awakening. Goosepimples prick his skin. His arm hair stands on end.

Two years.

Two god damn fucking years.

Nothing.

Not a squeak, not a sighting, nothing but taunts.

Until now.

But why? Why now?

No.

Can't think like that.

They almost have him.

"We're nearly there," Elizabeth announces. "ETA thirty seconds."

"Good. Kill the sirens, park out of sight."

Elizbeth brings the car to a halt in a housing estate, with the café hidden behind a patch of trees. Sean is out of the car before it's come to a complete halt, rushing toward the café's car park, where he sees his other offices concealed behind a set of trees.

He peers into the window of the café.

There he is.

Same pathetic dress sense. Bowtie. Braces. Checked shirt. Cream trousers. Looking like an inflated, demented child.

A sense of unease fills Sean's stomach.

It's like he's trying to tease, purposefully being noticeable.

Then it hits Sean like a brick in the face.

Why would he sit in the window of a café?

"This is too easy," Sean mutters to the other officers.

Why would he sit so obviously?

"Call the firearms unit," Sean instructs Elizabeth.

"Affirmative." She turns to her radio. "DC Elizabeth Hurks, requesting immediate firearm response at café on Dalton Road, please confirm."

Elizabeth awaits the response in her earphones, then turns to Sean.

"ETA thirty minutes," she says.

"Thirty minutes?" Sean responds with a scowl.

"This is Gloucestershire. Not London. We don't have firearms on standby, they need to assemble – thirty minutes is good."

Sean sighs, exasperated.

It's too easy.

Victor has something planned. He knows it.

Victor raises his hand to a nearby waitress, calling her over. The waitress returns a moment later with a receipt.

He's getting the bill.

He's leaving.

Sean can't do this. Can't let him go.

"We could tail him," Elizabeth offers, noticing the conundrum spread across his face.

"No, he'll lose us. He would come out with a plan."

"So what do we do?"

Sean looks down.

Thinks.

Racks his brain.

Fuck it.

"I'm going in."

"Okay." Elizabeth turns to prompt the other officers.

"No," Sean says, stopping her. "*I* am going in."

"Sean, come on."

"No, it's too easy. It's me he's taunting. I'll go in, see if I can make the arrest."

"We could surround the place within seconds, there'd be no way for him to leave."

"There'll always be a way. He always finds a way."

"He's not a wizard, Sean. He's just a man."

Sean turns to Elizabeth with a look of pure horror glued

to his expression with such rigidity it was like it had been moulded out of clay.

"Just a man?" he repeats. "*Just a man?* And that, Elizabeth, is why I am the one calling the shots. Hold your position until I call for backup."

Before Elizabeth can object, he marches forcefully across the car park without any intention to make an arrest.

Chapter Seven

Victor smiles at the waitress as she takes the money.

They've been holding that position for ages. But now they are advancing. Sean Mallon is walking toward him across the car park.

Brave man.

Foolish, but brave.

It makes Victor smile. It just shows how well Sean knows him. The fact that he doesn't send everyone in after him, but that Sean comes in alone.

That's why they are such good friends.

But it's not time yet. It's nowhere near time.

"Keep the change, dear," Victor says to the waitress with a wink.

He stands, places an envelope on the table, then turns to the window and makes eye contact with Sean.

Victor waves.

Then he leaves.

Chapter Eight

THE FUCKER.

The absolute fucking piece of shit!

He waved.

The bastard actually waved!

Sean feels his nails digging into his palms.

Victor stood. Turned. Walked further into the café.

Sean picks his pace up into a charging run.

"Elizabeth, he's heading for the back exit, get there now and see him off," he barks into his radio.

"Confirmed," is Elizabeth's reply.

He withdraws his Asp and kicks open the door. Startled faces turn to him as conversations abruptly cease, but Sean doesn't acknowledge it. His eyes turn directly to the vacant seat Victor Crane had occupied only moments ago.

"Everybody down!" he shouts, with such force his voice is a croaky growl that strains his throat. "Police, get down!"

Everyone obeys, ducking beneath their tables.

"Where is the waitress who served this table?" he demands. No one replies. "Where is the fucking waitress, tell me *now*!"

No one answers.

"There must have been a waitress that handed the guy sitting here the bill, where are you?"

A feeble hand is raised.

"Where did he go?"

She turns her quivering arm into a point directed behind her, toward the back of the café.

"Is that where the backdoor is?"

She nods.

"Elizabeth, what is your status?" he requests into his radio.

He sees an envelope left on the table as he passes Victor's empty coffee cup.

He ignores it. It'll be a taunt, he knows it. He'll see it later. Victor could still be here.

He directs his heavy, eager legs in the direction of the backdoor, punching everything open as he goes. Every door, every cupboard, every seat, every shadow, every space a person could occupy. He knocks himself against the walls, making no effort to be subtle.

He reaches the backdoor. It is a heavy fire door, but his leg doesn't care; he kicks it open and slams it against the wall.

There stands Elizabeth, along with other officers.

"You get him?"

She shakes her head.

He looks around. They are in an open area surrounded by fields and estates. No sight of Victor. He could be anywhere by now. In those seconds, he could have gone in any direction, in any vehicle.

"Search the surroundings," Sean instructs, refusing to give up. "Set up a perimeter blocking all cars, get someone in the station to monitor all nearby CCTV, track him, find where he went, what direction – we cannot let him escape."

Elizabeth nods and does as she is told.

There's no point.

Victor will have planned it. Foreseen it, from the timings of requesting his bill to knowing Sean well enough to predict he'd make the foolish drunken decision of coming in alone.

This only serves to highlight to Sean what he already knows; that he is losing it. That alcohol and anger are clouding his mind. What a ridiculous decision to make. What a pathetic, awful decision.

Still, he could beat himself up about it later.

He charged back into the café, looking around.

Everyone still remained beneath their tables, timidly awaiting their freedom.

He finds himself next to the envelope.

He opens it.

A picture. His ex-wife, her new husband, having tea with his young daughter. His young daughter sat in a wheelchair. Forever confined.

He turns the table over.

Everything smashes, but not enough. Everything has to break. Be destroyed.

Everything from the nearby tables goes. Every mug, glass, plate, saucer, spoon – everything is launched into the walls and reduced to pieces.

It's not enough. Everything needs to be torn apart. Everything needs to know how fucking god damn shitting angry he is.

"*FUCK!*"

With a violent scream, he kicks the chairs across the café, punches through the menus, slams his fists into the wall until they crack and dent.

Once there is nothing left to be bombarded he stands there, out of breath. Wondering why he still has his badge. Considering whether a fading reputation is enough to keep an inept, incompetent hazard on the pay check of Gloucestershire's finest.

He chooses to wait. Refusing to lose hope that Victor was still there. See if the perimeter stops him. If the CCTV can track him.

Any other person and they would.

But not Victor.

Sean is all too aware how incompetent this makes him sound. Like he thinks the bastard is magic, incapable of screwing up. He's had to face the same questions from the same media multiple times, and his answer is always the same:

If you think that it's simple, you just don't know Victor Crane.

He will send the photo left to taunt him for examination, but they will find nothing.

He has no idea how Victor does it, but he does.

Time after time after fucking time.

Sean knows people are watching him. Café customers, waitresses, his colleagues. Judging him. Arbitrating him as a disgrace to the police.

He does not care.

He just does not care.

Chapter Nine

August Daniels reaches the crime scene at nearly three in the afternoon. Always a consummate professional, he had called the Scene of Crime Officers straight away, and he arrives just as they are finishing. Police tape surrounds the family home, shutting it off from the public and the family who are still, apparently, on holiday.

As he steps out of the car he straightens his tie and tucks his shirt in. After sipping the rest of his coffee-to-go, he discards the cup into a nearby bin. The bin is almost full, so he pushes his cup in to ensure it does not get blown away in the breeze.

"Inspector," an officer acknowledges August, giving him a nod. August returns the nod and follows the officer to the crime scene.

August stops when he reaches the door to the house. He places on his white suit, making him look indistinguishable from the Scene of Crime Officers. He writes his name, notes the time and signs in, then proceeds into the house.

As he makes his way through the living room and the hallway, his head turns to look at the family home. To one side of him, pictures of children hang undisturbed up the stairs. To the other side, scenic photos of holidays gone sit atop cupboards. Occasional child's toys are left discarded on the furniture. This part of the house, at least, has not been meddled with.

"Has anyone let the family know?" August asks the nearest officer.

"Er, I think they are trying to get through to them, but not getting anything."

"Where are they?"

"Spain, I think."

August nods and allows the officer to carry on with his work.

He makes his way to the top of the basement. It is here where he first pauses to acknowledge the clues of death; a few flickers of blood around the doorway, and a handprint on the door visible under the strong UV lights erected behind him.

As he walks down the stairs, his light step creaking the wooden beams, the stench of death makes him choke. Then he sees the body.

Two wooden chairs face each other. One is empty, except for vacant ankle restraints left around the legs of the chair. Opposite, on the second chair, is Danielle Brooks. Her head is tilted to the side, displaying wide-open eyes and a hole in her forehead where the bullet passed through. Her body is bound in rope, her hands in handcuffs behind her back, and her ankles restrained.

A few Scene of Crime Officers flash their cameras whilst others place evidence in plastic bags, or take swabs from the remnants of blood and skin on the walls, chairs and restraints.

This is the third of these in the past few months, and August can't deny that he is beginning to feel that sense of unease all over again. Two chairs, one with looser restraints than the other, and only one dead body.

Why? There have clearly been two people here, so why only one body? Surely the killer didn't restrain themselves as well – unless that was part of their sexual thrill? But even that doesn't make sense. If it was part of a masochistic thrill he'd have expected to see more evidence of sexual assault, but there hadn't been such evidence on any of the victims.

Dealing with a serial killer in a small country city like Gloucestershire is very rare. Yet they had Victor Crane two years ago, and now this.

Are Gloucestershire police starting to look incompetent from their handling of the Victor Crane case? Do psychopaths see it as a weak spot?

Surely not with Sean Mallon in the station. Yes, he isn't what he used to be, but his achievements are still well known.

Honestly, August isn't sure where else to go with this investigation. Every line of enquiry has grown stale. Every piece of evidence led to nowhere. Every suspect has been released. Every piece of DNA matches up to no one they can find.

Frustratingly, August does know of a man who would know what to do next. A man, fallen from his pedestal, obsessed with chasing a single perpetrator on his own personal vendetta.

He won't help. August knows it.

Sean is dead set on another case. Dead set on his path to self-destruction. To the complete and utter annihilation of his liver and his mental state.

They used to be close.

Great friends. Great comrades. And even better colleagues.

They had achieved so much, despite not always getting on.

August needs his advice. He knows he can't solve this murder on his own.

He sighs.

He's not entirely sure what's more stressful — hunting serial killers or being Sean's superior.

He knows he can no longer rely on Sean — not like he used to, anyway. And he seems to spend his entire professional life defending Sean's digressions and poor decisions.

But beneath that is a brilliant man with a brilliant instinct, who perhaps just needs a more solvable case to restore that faith in him, not just from the department, but from himself.

He needs Sean Mallon's help.

But convincing him will be tough.

Dear Sean,

Oh, you are ever so much fun!

Did you find me? Or did I pick the perfect spot without traffic cameras, with a terrain I had spent months learning, in a situation I had planned long before you could ever know about?

You think you caught me in the allotment by chance?

I, of course, hope you realise why I did this.

If you do not, then please, allow me to enlighten you.

I did this to remind you that I am out of your reach. That you can set every police officer, every surveillance camera, and every dog on me that you wish – but you will still never ever, ever, ever catch me.

And I'm a little hurt that you don't realise this. I thought we had a deal. Yet, you are still hunting me. Still chasing shadows.

I hope the picture served as a good enough warning to show what will happen if you do not cease your investigation.

I have left you alone. I have left you and your crippled child to your own lives on the presumption that you would leave me to mine. I care for you, Sean, but I don't want to see you keep failing and failing – it is not good for you. Not for your mental health, or for you as a man.

If you want me to come back into your life and tear it apart, then I can. Taking away your daughter's use of her legs was merely a starter. I can rip through everyone and everything that you care about.

Trust me.

I can reach my hand into the filth of your existence, pull it away, and watch the strings of your life collapse around you. I can destroy your daughter, destroy your daughter's mother, and even destroy the man your daughter now calls father since your ridiculous existence has been pried from her memory.

I will maim your boss, August Daniels – the only thing standing between you and an expulsion from the police force that has already left you behind.

I will rape Elizabeth Hurks and make your daughter watch. I will lick her liver than stick my dick in your daughter's open heart. I will heave my warm, panting breath over her helplessly squirming body as I watch her beg for more, and laugh that she can't even kick out.

Then Carmen. Beautiful, lovely Carmen. I will penetrate her with a knife and unseam her from the nave to the chops like I was Macbeth. I will wrestle with her flesh the way a dog wrestles with a bone.

And then I will turn on you. Violate any woman you show affection for. Maim any acquaintance you so much as hint at making. Then I will tie you to a chair and make you watch everything as you beg me to stop.

Leave me be.

I really do miss you, Sean. But it is time for me to continue my life without you. And I know that, if you let go, you may even stand a chance of finding some happiness.

So, please, find that happiness. Become the man you once were. Become brilliant again.

I know how proud it would make me to see that.

With the bestest of wishes.

Your friend,

Victor Crane

Chapter Ten

SEAN STANDS AT A DISTANCE SO HE CAN'T BE SEEN.

In the shadows. Beneath an overhanging tree. Lurking silently, his black clothes disguising his ominous figure.

Even the estate is better than he is. A middle-class, suburban area. Happy families pour out of people carriers as they enter their homes with pictures of love adorning their windowsills. They carry out their blissful lives, loving each other, telling their kids off when they are naughty, hugging them when they cry, pretending they are unaware of the filth that lurks beneath their lives.

Sean has seen too many of these families torn apart by one little action of a selfish human being to have faith that their love and solidarity would ever be enough.

But he doesn't care. He's not here for them.

He's here for Lily.

He can see her through the window. Beautiful, long, blond hair just like her mother. She sits in her wheelchair at the tea table, knife and fork in her hands, awaiting her home-cooked meal.

Sean could never really cook. Sheila would always get

49

mad that he'd only ever make her microwave meals. Said he needed to learn. But Sean had always thought that there were more important things to learn in life.

Such as how to defend yourself against a killer.

Lily takes a bite. It looks like it's macaroni and cheese. She smiles. She loves it. She's happy.

Sheila walks in and sits beside her. Her belly is big. It looks like she's pregnant again.

Good for her.

No, really, good for her.

Lily would be a great older sister.

Paul enters. Wearing a neat suit. A well-groomed beard. Hair combed to the side.

He puts his arms around Sean's daughter's shoulders and Sean's heart beats faster, cracking, breaking into a million pieces. Paul kisses her gently on the forehead and she looks up at him with eyes of adoration. She looks up at him like he is her father.

It still hurts. The memory. Holding the biro in his hand as he places his signature on the bottom line. Then the paper was whisked away and it was done. No more to do. No more to say. She was gone.

There was no legal right, or ethical right, for him to be in her life.

It was the best decision for Lily.

Sean reminds himself of that.

Lily needs a man better than he to be her father. A man who would never put her in danger simply by existing. A man who didn't have death follow him wherever he went.

Lily's adoptive father strokes his hand down her hair as he takes his place at the head of the table.

I once sat there. Long ago…

Lily talks to him, and he talks to her, a smile on his face, the smile only a true father can have. Looking at his daughter.

At Sean's daughter.

Sean gave Paul custardy. Now she doesn't even know who Sean is. Gone. Forgotten. Discarded like yesterday's Sunday roast.

Fourteen years old now. Everything to live for. A happy family.

This is something Sean could never give her.

A truly devoted parent does what's best for their kid.

Giving her a new father was best for her.

She doesn't need some lazy alcoholic layabout obsessed with catching a serial killer that he will never catch.

Lily finishes her tea. Paul stands up and places his hands on the bars of her wheelchair, taking her out of the room. She disappears out of sight then appears in the living room. Paul puts his arms beneath her and carries her from the wheelchair to the sofa, where he places her down and puts on the television. She smiles and laughs while he does this.

Paul then helps his pregnant wife to her seat.

He is a good man. A brilliant man. Great dad, great husband.

Paul is what Sean could never be, and that is why Paul is such a good man.

Sean is the reason she has to be taken to the living room in a wheelchair and carried to the sofa. Because he let Victor Crane into his life, and that meant his daughter had to pay the price. But she laughs when Paul helps her. Laughs and jokes and smiles like it's nothing.

I did that to her.

No.

Victor Crane did that to her.

He abducted her. Abducted Sean. Made Sean choose between capturing Victor and saving his daughter.

Victor left her bleeding in his arms.

This is what remains.

Believing Sean no longer exists is her salvation.

He can't see what they are watching, what is on television, but she's laughing, smiling and laughing and joking and looking adoringly at Paul and it kills Sean, kills every piece of him, twists his insides into a million knots and pulls them up through his throat until he's choking, choking the last piece of life out of him.

It kills him.

He hates that he's not that man for her. He hates that some other prick gets to be him. But most of all, he knows that the other prick is not a prick. He's incredible. He is everything his family needs him to be.

And Sean is not.

He takes out a flask of whiskey.

What a cliché. Like some victim of a 1940s film noir. The helpless detective chugging on whiskey. The hero who was never a hero.

But it's different to live it.

If living is what he's doing.

For a moment he wonders, *am I even alive?* He feels dead. Like he's falling, spiralling down a dark hole, and now he's landed, and he's staring, looking upwards, toward the black abyss of the pit he could never climb out of.

I love you, Lily.

Even that name. Lily.

Sean and Sheila named her Charlotte.

Sheila changed that name.

Changed it so Sean couldn't find her.

She's better off with him. They all are.

He places the flask of whiskey back inside his pocket. Turns away. Walks down the street. His car awaits him around the corner, out of the way so he doesn't attract attention.

A man glances at Sean out of his window.

What the hell are you looking at?

He could take him.

He could take anyone.

Just watch me.

He bows his head. He's pathetic. Deluded. Mentally challenging a guy to a fight because he's curious about a suspicious bloke hanging around his family home.

It's all his fault.

No, it's Victor Crane's fault.

He'll get him.

He will.

I love you, Lily.

Though she'll never know, he had her best interests in the core his heart.

Chapter Eleven

THERE'S ALWAYS A VICTIM AND A VILLAIN.

That's how the murders work.

It's about redemption, see.

I abduct both of them. The victim, and the villain.

The villain has always been wronged somehow, and the victim is the damned. In need of redemption.

And I give it to them.

The villain is tied up. The victim gets the weapon. They get to point it and see what happens.

And that is what happened.

Danielle Brooks had wronged Danny. She had stolen his father's watch, a very treasured watch, and she had pawned it for a weekend's worth of alcohol and cocaine.

I gave Danny the gun, gave Danielle the seat, and offered him redemption.

And he took it.

Damn, he took it.

But this isn't it, see.

This is just practice.

All of them so far have been practice.

Because I need to get it right.

Get ready for the biggy.

Oh, it's going to be a biggy.

Just wait for it.

And now I have the next pair ready to practice with.

Then maybe there'll be a next one. And another, and another, and another – *until I feel ready.*

None of them counts until the biggy.

By then, it won't even matter if they realise who I am. It doesn't count until they know. And they have to know.

Danielle was a try-out. Amateur league.

I can't be doing with explaining this to you, you're just going to have to believe me.

There is a very particular process to this.

You think murders just happen on a whim?

You could not be more wrong.

It's like a cooking recipe. There are ingredients. Instructions. Method.

All stirred into the final result.

A good death takes time. Takes precision, perfecting, pre-empting.

It's an art.

And I'm an artist.

Just like he is.

I am doing this all for him.

Chapter Twelve

The familiar rhythmless ringtone of Sean's mobile phone prompts him to stir from his slumber.

He lifts his head and he can already feel the imprint of the steering wheel upon his face.

He looks around.

The café car park. He's still there. Everyone else has left, but he is still there. The last place Victor Crane was sighted. Where the bastard waved at him.

Sean doesn't want to leave. If he leaves then it means the chance was over

The phone stops ringing. Sean's throbbing headache is relieved.

How could all the other officers have just left him there to sleep?

He had watched them from his car as they did their examinations, did their photographs, did their search of the area, operated a perimeter – but the clarity of the afternoon had now turned to dark and Sean was the only person that remained.

That's the thing about being an alcoholic. The uncontrollable naps in the middle of the afternoon. One minute you are overseeing an operation then, before you know it, your head is lolling and your eyes are drooping.

Either the rest of the officers didn't notice he was asleep – or, they decided to leave his pathetic self to his impromptu nap.

It doesn't even hurt that everyone else thinks of him as pathetic. As pitiful. As a joke. He is numb to it. He already has enough to be angry about.

He sighs. Rubs the sleep out of his eyes. Decides he better go back to the station and see what has been found – though it would likely be fuck-all.

It's the same every time.

He has done this song and dance multiple times over the past few years.

He taunts you.

You fall for it.

You find nothing.

It's the way it always happens.

His phone rings again.

"What?" he grunts down it, still rubbing his face, cursing the moon for being so damn bright.

"Sean, it's August."

"What do you want?"

"I need your help. Can you come to Dalton Street?"

He glances at his watch. He isn't wearing one. Just a naked wrist with the indent of a watch.

"Why?"

"I just need your help. Come on, Sean, do me a favour."

A big sigh fills his lungs and pours out of him.

"Fine."

He hangs up.

Whatever you say, August.

Whatever you want, August.

Sean knows he owes a lot to that man, a man who has taken a lot of slack for being Sean's boss – slack that has been entirely deserved. Sean is convinced August only puts up with him on the basis that Sean is good at what he does.

Which is wrong.

He *used* to be good at what he does.

He *used* to be fucking brilliant at what he does.

But the guy insists on calling him every time a dead body shows up. Like August can't solve a murder without him. Like Sean's opinion is the only one August listens to.

Silly August.

In the MET, murder was a way of life. Something that happened every day, due to a gang, a psycho, a robbery, or whatever whino tried nicking something and ended up going horribly wrong.

But in the country, in the middle of bloody nowhere, his colleagues aren't as accustomed to the sight of a corpse as those London. They don't have a sodding clue what to do.

Sean arrives at Dalton Street and goes to undo his seatbelt – notices that he forgot to put it on – and drags himself out of the car.

As he arrives at the door to a family home he is instructed to put on one of the white hazard suits so he looks like the Scene of Crime Officers. He huffs. What does it actually do? Like one of his hairs are going to fall onto the victim and suddenly his DNA and the murder's DNA mixes and mutates into some giant loser.

He signs his name, puts his suit on, hesitantly going along with the same pointless routine. He is directed down the weak basement stairs where August stands beside a dead body. A bullet hole is in the forehead of the corpse and her body is restrained to a chair, opposite a vacant seat.

August turns to Sean. For a moment his eyes hover, and Sean can see August trying to cover his repulsion at the sight of what his friend has become; the greasy hair, the messy beard, the stench of booze. To be fair to him, August does it well.

"So what do you think, Sean?"

Sean shakes his head awake and surveys the room.

"Gee, it looks like she was shot through the head."

Sean turns to leave. Case closed. Not bloody rocket science, is it?

"Sean, wait," August requests and Sean stops. His head pounds. Nicotine withdrawal makes his arms shake.

"What?" he says, trying to open his eyes beyond a squint. The artificial light that stands in the corner illuminating the crime scene is far too bright for his eyes.

"We have a few theories, care to entertain us?" August hopefully requests.

"August, I've got–"

"Nothing to do, I bet."

Sean says nothing.

"Humour me."

Sean shrugs. Whatever.

"Laurence," August shouts out, and a small walking blob wobbles over to them. Laurence looks like the last person you would want to arrive at a crime scene. His greasy hair is combed over to cover his balding head, acne is sporadically placed over his cheeks, and he seems to talk like every word comes from the bottom of his throat.

"Hi, it's great to finally meet you," Laurence introduces himself. "I'm DC Laurence Kinney."

Laurence offers his hand but Sean looks at it like he's offering shit on a cake.

"How about you just tell him your hypothesis?" August prompts.

This should be good.

"Well, since there is a chair opposite her that has so far

shown signs of DNA that isn't hers, we suppose that she wasn't alone. I think she was trapped with a friend, and her friend got loose, escaped, then was caught by the killer further outside or something – we are yet to finish surveying the area. We believe that the killer put them here days ago and left them to either starve or shoot the other to escape. We have no reason to believe the abductor was in the room with them for much of it, or even for the death, considering they may not have been the one to fire the bullet."

Laurence smirks like he just won a spelling contest in front of his classmates. His chin fat wobbles with his grin, as does the waddle on his throat, that disgusting bit of hanging skin blokes who let themselves go always get.

It both fascinates Sean and makes him want to gag. How does a bloke like this actually pass the police fitness test?

Shit, how do I pass the fitness test? Shouldn't I be taking one of those…

"What do you think, Sean?" August asks, waiting for Sean to endow this idiot with praise.

Sean rubs his sinus. He could really do with a drink.

"Which bit?" Sean asks. "The pointless load of waffle I just heard, or the fact that it's all utter bollocks?"

Laurence looks like Sean had just smacked his cat and pissed on his front lawn.

"Care to enlighten us?" August prompts.

"So," Sean starts, forcing himself to talk, despite the energy it takes to have to turn his thoughts into words. "You think that the abductor wasn't in the room with them when they died?"

Laurence nods.

"You are adamant of that?"

"It's a possibility," Laurence weakly replies.

Sean sighs. "Both of the victims were barefoot."

"How could you possibly know that?"

"Because these ankle restraints are leather padded posture restraints," Sean says, pointing at the vacant restrains beside the empty seat. "They are bigger than the average restraints, meaning that they not only go over their ankle but also over their foot. It wouldn't fit on them if they were wearing shoes – and you can see our corpse here is not wearing shoes either. Correct?"

Laurence looks down, his mouth hanging dumbly open.

"Er, yes, I guess."

Sean walks to behind the vacant chair and points at a trail of wet boot prints leading to the stairs.

"These still glisten. They are recent. Like, within the last twelve hours. When did you estimate the murder happened, August?"

"Between 10.00 p.m. and midnight."

"So we have established that the killer must have been in here at that time then, yes?"

Laurence shakes his head like he's shaking himself out of a bad dream.

"Er… yeah."

"Yes?" Sean awaits more of a response. He sees August smirking. Enjoying this as much as Sean would be if he wasn't dying for a drink.

"How long have you been working as a detective?"

"Er, a few years."

"Right." Sean turns to August. "I'm going for a slash. Got a commode in this place?"

Sean walks up the stairs, out of the house, pushing the ridiculous outfit off with as much energy as he can muster.

Before he reaches his car, August has caught up with him.

"Sean, wait."

"What?"

Sean normally had time for August, but at this moment,

he could not be arsed. He wants to know what Elizabeth whatsername found about Victor Crane.

"I need your help."

"It's a murder, August. Solve it. You don't need me."

"It's not a murder, Sean, it's a serial killer."

"How'd you know?"

"Because this is the third death under the exact same conditions that we have found in the last few months. It's a pattern."

Sean sighs. He's not doing it.

"You tested DNA? Done all that?"

"It matches on each crime scene. But beyond that, we have nothing. We've gone down every line of inquiry and nothing."

"Sounds like you've got a tricky case there."

Sean gets into his car.

"Sean, listen–"

"Jesus Bloody Christ, August, why are you trying to do this to me?"

"Do what to you? No one knows this type of case like you. You can stay on the Crane case, I just need some help, some advice–"

"Goodbye, August."

He turns on his engine.

"Come on, Sean. There's more to life than your desperate search for vengeance."

Now that stung.

Sean drives away, music loud enough that he doesn't hear the tyres screech.

Chapter Thirteen

TOBY ABRUPTLY SHOVES HIS MOBILE PHONE BACK IN HIS pocket as Lois re-enters the room.

"And you're going to be fine picking the kids up from school?" she continues, incessantly on and on, the same nagging questions, the same ridiculous inferences that Toby is an idiot, with no idea how to even get dressed in the morning.

"Yes, I know how to take our kids to school."

"And you know where I left the lasagne for tea?"

"Yes," he answers blandly.

"Do you, Toby?"

His hands grip the insides of his pockets.

"Christ, Lois, I'm a grown man and a father."

She raises her eyebrows as if to say… *I don't know. I don't know what she is trying to say.*

She makes him feel inept. Pathetic.

And I hate her for it.

"I'm just going to pop to the loo before I go."

"You do that."

She leaves the room.

He takes out his phone.

> She's going away tonight. The kids will be in
> bed by eight. You free? X x x x

HE FINISHES his text and watches the toilet door with avid eyes, awaiting the undoing of the lock. He can hear the faint sound of her urinating, and he knows he has a little more time.

His phone beeps and he practically bounces out his hands he's so excited.

> Looking forward to it ;) x x x x x x x x

THE TOILET FLUSHES.

He locks his phone. Pushes it back into the depths of his pocket. Quickly quells his excited smile.

She walks back into the kitchen, talking to herself in that irritating under-her-voice whisper she always uses when checking if she has everything, where she asks herself questions then answers them. This could possibly be what Toby hates most about her, after her continual patronising treatment of him.

"Do I have my keys? Yes, I do. Do I have my lunch? I think so. Is my phone in my pocket? Yes, it is."

He craves the feel of his hands around her throat.

He has no doubt whatsoever that Lois's sister is not needing Lois to visit her and comfort her about her god-awful marriage, but that Lois is off to fornicate with some guy somewhere else.

Or not. Because maybe he's the arsehole.

And I really don't care.

"Oh, I do hope it's not piddling down."

Piddling down?

What the fuck is 'piddling down'?

On second thought, he decides he isn't the arsehole. He's just a man who can't stand being married to an insufferable wretch any longer.

She puts her hand on her handbag.

"Handbag, check!" she sings, going high-pitched on the word *check* in a way that makes Toby shake with rage.

She puts her hand in her pocket.

"Phone, check!"

I could shoot you right now.

She puts her hands gently upon his face.

"Kiss with my husband."

She kisses him.

"Check!"

He wipes the kiss off on his sleeve when she turns around. It was sloppy and made half his face wet.

"I'm so sorry I have to go away again," she tells him, with a hint of fake sincerity in her voice. "My sister just can't catch a break. I think she's getting divorced."

Lucky her.

"Oh, how rubbish," Toby says. "I'll be fine. The kids will be fine. Don't worry."

"You sure you'll be fine making tea?"

"Yep."

"And you sure you'll be fine taking care of the kiddies without me?"

Oh my bloody god would you just go!

"Yep, pretty sure I can handle it."

Take care of the kiddies?

I'm their fucking father!

He'd changed them, fed them, read to them, helped them, consoled them, parented them – just as much as this stupid wench has.

"I will be fine," he reassures her, plastering a fake grin across his face, hoping that she doesn't try to kiss him again.

"I love you," she tells him, opening the front door and crossing the threshold. He closes the door behind her before she can force him to respond with the same lie.

He looks at the clock.

Six hours until she gets there.

Six hours that can't come soon enough.

Chapter Fourteen

IT'S THE SAME ROUTINE SEAN GOES THROUGH EVERY TIME HE passes through prison security. Patted down, searched, stripped of electric devices.

His mobile phone waits for him on the way out.

Good. I don't want to be disturbed.

He makes his way to the visitor's room where he hovers in the doorway. Scans faces. Recognises one or two as people that he put in prison, though that would have been a long time ago now. So long ago it feels like a different person did it. These criminals probably wouldn't even recognise his bristly unkept face and pale skin beneath his messy clump of greasy hair.

Sean sees him waiting. He walks over.

He's brought chocolate. They don't say a word for a few minutes as Sean takes a few bars out of a plastic bag and places them on the table.

"Hi, Jack," Sean finally greets him, watching him warily.

Jack scans his eyes over the chocolate bars and decides on a Mars, which he eats as if he hasn't eaten in days.

"Hello," he returns through mouthfuls of a chocolate bar.

Strange, really. That Sean visits Jack but hunts Victor. If you were to be on the outside looking in, it would look odd – Sean knew that. But it was different.

Jack had been Sean's mentee – or so Sean had thought. In truth, Jack had turned out to be the mentee of the murderous paedophile that Sean had killed. In revenge, Jack had leant himself to Victor's guidance, and together they caught both Sean and Sean's daughter. When the police got there, they managed to arrest Jack, but not Victor.

One could logically conclude that Jack was equally guilty of causing Sean's daughter's life-changing injuries as Victor was.

But it's different. Or, at least, Sean insists that it is.

Sean understands Jack, even if he doesn't agree with him.

Sean killed Jack's original mentor, Alexander Shirlov. What's more, he did it in cold blood and covered it up – something his colleagues are still unaware of today.

Whoever Shirlov was or what he did, Sean had struggled to come to terms with this. In a way, Jack was justified in his actions. Sean had unethically murdered his mentor, and he deserved a comeuppance.

Victor is different. He's a deranged psychopath who manipulated Jack. He has no other motive than death and chaos.

"So how you been?" Jack asks as he finishes the chocolate bar and licks the wrapper clean.

Sean drops his head.

I suppose I'm kidding myself.

Is he there because he understands Jack? Or is he just lonely? Jack is most likely the only person in the world Sean can talk openly and honestly with. The only person who does not disguise who they are or what has happened between them, however disgraceful their history may have been.

I'm so pathetic.

Ridiculous.

Get a grip.

"Not bad," Sean tells him, though he knows Jack doesn't buy it.

"Oh yeah? That why your clothes stink of booze? Why your breath reeks of it?"

"Yeah… How are you doing, Jack?"

Jack shrugs. "Best as I can be. How's the hunt for Victor?"

A release of air huffs out of Sean in an inexplicable, exaggerated noise.

"About as well as it was. Had another near miss. Like they all are."

Jack nods. Sean doesn't need to explain to him how smart Victor is. They both know Victor is a genius, in his own sick, twisted, demented way.

"Why don't you take a new case?" Jack asks. "Get some distance. Might help give you a bit of clarity."

Sean snorts. "Funny you should say that. August has come at me with another one."

"Take it."

Sean shakes his head.

"Nah. No point. The only reason I'm still here is for Victor."

"Yeah, and taking on a new case will help with that. You've been overloaded with Victor Crane for years – maybe a bit of distance will give you some fresh thoughts to return to it with. Think in the long term."

Maybe he's right.

Sean can't help but laugh.

Of all the people to give him good advice.

"Tell me about it," Jack prompts. "Maybe I can help."

"Potential serial killer, each victim found on a chair dead, facing an empty chair. Signs of someone being on that empty chair but left, and a third party we assume was the abductor."

"Sounds like something is being set up. Like the abductor might be getting the person in the empty seat to do his work under duress."

Yes. Of course. It makes sense.

"Wow, Jack. Shame what happened happened. You'd have been a crackin' detective."

An awkward silence descends, but only fleetingly.

"Maybe there's more of a motive to who they pick as well. Like he's offering them something. Something everybody wants. Something that's enough to make them kill another human being."

"Such as?"

Jack looks Sean dead in the eyes. "Redemption."

Sean nods.

"A redemption killer," Sean mulls over to himself. "Thanks."

Sean makes a decision.

Maybe Jack is right.

Maybe August needs help.

Maybe this is what he needs to clear his head.

Maybe–

No.

Victor.

That is all I care about now.

Chapter Fifteen

TOBY AWAKENS TO A VAST OPEN SPACE. IT'S DARK. HIS EYES struggle to adjust. His thoughts struggle to comprehend his surroundings.

It's a factory. Or was a factory. It's empty. A large, empty warehouse.

But why is he there?

He looks down. His body is restrained. He can't move anything but his head and neck. Rope wraps around his chest. Metallic casing squeezes uncomfortably against his wrists. His ankles are restrained to the chair over bare feet.

He's not alone.

Across from him is a woman. A woman he knows. A woman…

Lois.

His wife.

"Lois?" Toby asks.

She ignores him.

She isn't restrained like he is. Her legs are fastened to the chair, but that's it.

But her eyes are wet. Dried tears stain her cheek. She is distraught.

"Lois?" he tries again.

She shakes her head.

She's holding something in her lap. Pictures. He recognises himself in them.

"What are the pictures?" he persists. "What's going on?"

She lifts the pictures so he can see them.

Behind the wooden beams of a window is Toby sitting on a bed. A naked woman on her knees in front of him. Her mouth wrapped around his penis.

Beneath that, another picture of his naked backside as he thrusts into a woman on all fours before him.

Another of the same woman laid down on the bed, her legs wrapped around his neck, grabbing the bedsheets, her face caught in a moment of pleasure.

They continue and continue and continue. All positions, all sins, all guilty pleasurable looks upon the faces.

"Lois…" he whimpers.

He looks down at his predicament once more, then looks back at Lois's loose confines.

"Have you done this?" he requests.

"No," Lois finally responds. "No, I haven't."

Someone appears. Faint footsteps echo around a silhouette in the shadows. They grow closer, gaining on them.

Their face is covered. They are adorned in black, their identity disguised.

They place a knife in his wife's lap.

"What's going on?" Toby asks. He knows from the sound of his voice that he's scared; it quivers, shakes, lacking any assertiveness, replaced by terror and worry.

"Wh – what is this?" Lois asks.

"Redemption," replies the anonymous person.

"What – what are you talking about?"

They crouch beside Lois and whisper in her ear.

Toby struggles to make out what they say, but he catches three distinct words amongst them all: "slit his throat."

His whole body tenses.

Surely, she won't.

This is his wife.

She wouldn't.

Would she?

What would I do?

He refuses to answer himself that question.

"I – I can't," Lois stutters.

Toby breathes a temporary sigh of relief.

"Then I will slit yours," they reply, then take a few steps back, sinking back into the shadows, watching. A sick voyeur. Peering at Lois just as Toby does, watching the flickers of conflict spread across her face.

It's her life or his.

And he's the one who wronged her. Who cheated on her. Out of the both of them, he deserves it most.

But surely this is too extreme? *Surely I don't deserve to die?*

She looks at the knife laid in her hands, next to the pictures that prompt another pant of grief. Her arms are shaking, vigorously seizing. Her shoulders are hunched, tense. Her head shakes. Her lip quivers. Tears drip from the corner of her eyes into a lazy puddle, smashing the stone floor with a silent echo.

"Lois, please," he begs, seeing an unwanted conclusion start to meet her expression.

She looks to him. To the knife. To the photos. To him. To the photos.

The images of him naked, pleasuring another woman and being pleasured in turn.

"Lois, I know you won't kill me… We've had our problems, but I know you won't kill me…"

Except he doesn't. He doesn't know that. She may well kill him.

It's either her or her adulterous bastard of a husband.

She is still caught in the despair of discovering the infidelities. Her emotions cloud her judgement, creating a reckless clarity.

But she's not capable of it, he tells himself. She wouldn't have it in her. She's a pushover. A mother. A weak excuse for a human being.

But he deserves it. In her eyes, he deserves it.

All the battling, the fighting, the swearing, the going behind her back, the insipid remarks, the backhanded insults, the nights laying in bed facing the opposite direction. They had grown apart. They had barely touched each other's bodies in months.

Cheating was inevitable.

The affair came naturally.

One of them was bound to do it.

It just happened to be me.

It was luck, more than anything.

"Lois, just put the knife down," he pleads.

He sees her resolve dropping. Her face growing weaker. She won't do it, he knows she won't.

"I – I can't," she mutters, dropping the knife to the floor with a mighty clatter and covering her face.

Their captor walks over.

"Is that your decision?" they demand.

She shakes her head, covering her face, suppressing the desperate sobs.

"I can't…" she repeats.

Their captor wastes no time. Within seconds, the knife is lifted and dragged across his wife's throat.

Blood sprays like a broken tap.

He is forced to look into her wide eyes as she panics. As she begins to understand that she is about to die.

"Lois!"

He watches her.

She watches him.

They share eye contact, knowing there is nothing they can do.

They shared a family together. They shared a bed. Now they are sharing her death.

Eventually, she stops struggling.

He is left still staring at the corpse of his wife.

He throws up. Over his lap, on his feet, on the floor.

Their captor is behind Toby, speaking on the phone.

"Hello, I would like to report a murder."

Then the footsteps grow distant.

He is alone.

Alone with his wife.

Just watching her dead body flop helplessly to the side and collapse in a bloody heap on the floor.

Chapter Sixteen

NOTHING.

Diggly squat.

Bugger all.

Jack shit.

That is what they found.

No tyre tracks. No CCTV. No shadow to chase.

Victor had set this up with a plan to escape untracked, and he'd executed it perfectly.

How?

How the hell can someone do something like that?

How can someone possibly be this smart? Always be ahead of him?

Sean was supposed to be a sodding legend, and this guy was exposing him for the fraud he was.

It would have all been organised, thought through – Sean knows that. Planned months in advance. Victor teased them by leaving behind a leaf from his tyre. His escape route had been prepared and disguised in a way that meant Sean would not be able to find it.

Sean was useless. A charlatan. Inept.

How does Victor manage to do this?

As soon as he re-enters the designated case room he launches a whiskey glass at the wall and turns his chair upside down. Then he feels ridiculous for another childish stroppy tantrum. Then he doesn't care.

He just doesn't care.

It's humiliating.

This is what he lives for. What he waits for. He wants it all to be over, but this prick keeps doing this.

Every time he thinks he's close…

Every bloody time…

Sean sees August in the doorway.

Sean stands there, panting, willing his breathing to subside. Feeling more and more stupid that he's being watched.

"How long you been stood there?" Sean asks.

"Long enough," August replies.

Thanks, August. *Make me feel even more of a dick, why don't you?*

"There's been another killing," August tells Sean. "Same pattern. Same killer."

Sean exhales his frustration as he lifts his head to the sky, only to see a stained, crumbling ceiling. His legs feel heavy, his body feels old, his mind feels worn. He can't do this anymore. He can't keep doing this.

"We could do with your help," August insists.

"You don't need my help," Sean responds with a low pitch and quiet volume, leaning over a chair with his head dropped and his eyes momentarily closed. "I don't know anything."

"You knew enough to identify the abductor was in the room in the last crime scene. You knew that within seconds of being there. Imagine what you could do within minutes. Within hours."

"August, I'm no good at this."

"How about I'll decide whether you're too good or not?"

"Jesus Christ, August."

Get the message.

I want to be left alone.

But then again…

Do I? Do I really want to be left alone? Left to sit and stew and wallow in self-pity?

Jack's advice repeats itself in Sean's thoughts.

"Come on," August continues. "Get your coat."

Sean hesitates.

"Sean, trust me, you'll want to be here for this – there's a survivor."

"Fine."

Sean gets his coat and follows.

Dear Sean,

Old friends. That's what we are. Do you feel that too? Like we've known each other our whole lives? I do.

I feel like we could stay up all night talking. I could reminisce about the people I've killed, you about the one that you've killed. We could discuss why I do what I do, why you do what you do. We could really get to grips with each other. Understand each other.

I feel like we would fascinate each other.

That's probably the reason you pursue me in the same way I sometimes pursue you.

Not because I crippled your daughter. That's just your excuse.

It's fascination.

Complete, undeniable, incontrovertible fascination.

I am captivated with trying to understand your motivations. Why do you keep pursuing me? Why do you fall for every trap, every wrong turn, every taunt? Do you love being humiliated?

Or maybe I'm all you live for.

You probably don't even care about what I did to your daughter. It just sparked your desire for vengeance, and that is what gives your existence a point. A purpose. A reason.

Maybe you are, on a sub-conscious level, purposefully being a lousy detective, so you don't catch me, and end up without purpose.

Well, you give my life purpose too, Sean.

And guess what?

I'm going to start killing again.

If you do not leave me alone then the bodies will pile up. I will send their remains to your address. Imagine reading my letter over breakfast accompanied by the ear of a nine-year-old girl.

Those are my favourites, nine-year-olds. There's something so innocent about that age.

It's like when you chase a criminal in your police car and their driving gets reckless, and yours becomes dangerous, and chasing them means you are going to endanger lives, so you have to stop the chase and let them go. That's why are you going to stop chasing me now: to prevent more deaths.

Although my hands will be the murder weapon, you will be the one killing them. Because you didn't heed my warning.

Although, chances are, without your hunt for me, you will find yourself with no reason to go on. No reason to drag yourself out of your bed in the morning. No reason to force yourself to battle through your alcoholic mess of a mind and make yourself sit in that same empty chair every minute of every day, staring at clues that tell you nothing. I'm doing this for your own good, Sean, you need to re-evaluate.

We are friends, aren't we?

I think we are. Good friends. Best friends, almost.

So, as your friend, let me give you a piece of advice.

Just end it.

Put us all out of our misery.

End this pointless existence, cease your agony, halt your aimless wandering through this world. It would do you a favour, and everyone else around you. You would never have to put up with your snivelling, pathetic ways again.

And then your daughter will be truly safe.

Because that is who I will finish with.

If you don't stop.

You think what I did to her before was bad?

There is no way to put a laugh in a letter, Sean, but if I could, I would be doing that now. A nice, hearty laugh, like the Ghost of Christmas Present. Or of a jolly giant from a jolly story.

If you think about it, this all makes sense.
After all, I am doing this for you, Sean.
You are warned.
Missing you as always, and sending you happy thoughts.
Your friend,
Victor Crane

Chapter Seventeen

THE SCENE IS SIMILAR TO BEFORE. ALMOST IDENTICAL, EVEN. Except, this time there is a body next to the ankle restraints and a man blubbering endless words of terror.

That's the first thing Sean notices – that the setup is the same, but the survivor is different.

August goes to send the man to the hospital, but Sean stops him.

"Get him checked over by a doctor here, we can't let him go."

"Why?" August asks, looking at Sean quizzically.

"Because he's the only survivor."

"We will send officers with him."

"No, August, he's a suspect, we need to talk to him."

"A suspect, Sean? Look at him!"

"Yes, he's probably not the killer, but we need to rule him out."

August hesitates.

"You brought me here for my advice," Sean reminds August. "I can go whenever I want. You want my help, that's what I ask."

Sean makes his way outside for some air. He lights a cigarette and enjoys its warm taste as its smoke caresses his lungs.

Elizabeth gets out of the car and walks toward him.

"Anything?" he asks, having left her in charge of pursuing any clues that may arise from further analysis of the café, however helplessly hopeful such a request is.

She solemnly shakes her head.

He's gutted, but not surprised.

"How does he keep doing this?" Elizabeth asks.

Sean shrugs.

"We've checked CCTV from everywhere within a ten-mile radius," Elizabeth continues. "We're eighty percent through, more or less. Nothing."

Sean feels momentarily hopeful that they still had twenty percent left, but the hope fades as he acknowledges to himself that it is futile.

He bows his head. She doesn't know about the letters. About the threats. He keeps them to himself.

Like he kept the phone calls to himself two years ago.

Jesus. Two years?

It's a long time. And it was a stupid move then, as it is a stupid move now, but he doesn't see the use in declaring it. They would probably take him off the case.

He's not a detective. To them, sure, he is – but to him, he's just letting them think he's a detective so he can use their resources.

He stopped being a real policeman a long time ago.

"I think this is good," Elizabeth announces.

"What?" Sean looks around himself. "Another death?"

"No, I mean, you working on something else. Clearing your head. I think it helps."

"Fucking Jesus, Elizabeth, join the soddin' choir."

Sean humphs and turns away from her, barking at a subordinate to get him a damn coffee.

He withdraws his phone and texts Carmen. He wants her in his flat tonight. He needs to feel her closeness. He doesn't care how much it costs, he just needs her skin against his.

Even if she's obliging just because she likes money.

He can pretend for a few hours it's not so.

I'm so sad.

He has to pay someone to hold him. Sure, he fucks her, but that's just because he can – what he craves is her. The feel of a body around his. The intimacy of love.

August appears at his side.

"We got a name?" Sean asks.

"Toby Marshall," August replies. "Father of two. The deceased is his wife, Lois Marshall. There were pictures by his feet."

"Pictures of what?"

"Taken through a window of what appears to be Toby Marshall having an affair."

Sean nods. Jack was right. Spot on with his reading of the situation. Shame his path went wayward, he would be a brilliant asset.

"What are you thinking?" August asks.

"It's a redemption killer. They get someone who wronged someone else, and tell them to either kill that person or be killed themselves – as if this is an offer of redemption."

"That's a hell of a hypothesis, Sean."

Sean doesn't tell August where the notion came from. The mind of a sick killer can always understand sick killers better than the rest of them could.

"Think about it, August. The killer gets two people, and only one of them dies. And one of them has these photos.

It's so set up. Get Toby Marshall, see if he can confirm any of this."

"We'll be a few minutes, we're setting up an interrogation room."

"Quickly, August, time is of the essence."

Jesus, do I hear myself?

He scoffs.

'Time is of the essence.'

Still, it feels good to actually be doing something real for once.

The Purpose

Chapter Eighteen

It's eight years ago and August is twenty-six. He's already a sergeant, and Sean is already a detective. They are two of the most talented officers the station have seen in a long time – or so their inspector says. And they are on a case together. And they are killing it.

"Tell us again where you were on Friday?" Graham Shooter, the seasoned interrogator asks.

"No comment," replies the overweight, acne-ridden paedophile sitting opposite them with his smug lawyer and his tubby arms folded like two fat loaves of bread.

"If you don't tell us, then–"

"No comment." The guy even interrupts this time.

Behind the one-way window, August and Sean exchange worried glances. They know this guy is guilty. They don't just feel it in their bones, they see it in the suspect's eyes. That cockiness he always has, knowing that they haven't enough evidence, knowing that he will escape being charged for the umpteenth time.

"We have a witness who says they saw you at the off-licence at 8.23 p.m., now if–"

"That witness's testimony," interrupts the lawyer, "Has already been found to be uncorroborated, and it has been agreed that it will be wiped from the record."

Graham shakes his head.

"Do you not have anything to say about this testimony before it's stricken?" Graham directs at the narcissistic, obese fiend.

"No comment," he repeats, then adds a little wink to it.

"We're fucked," August announces.

Sean strokes his chin. Thinks. They can't let him go. It's their first big case and they have nothing. They all know he's the perpetrator, but as it stands they are going to have to let him go, leaving him to undoubtedly offend again.

"Thoughts?" August asks, seeing that Sean is deep in thought.

"It's tricky," Sean quietly agrees.

"Tricky? It's not tricky, it's impossible. We have an unreliable witness, CCTV that places him in the town centre on the evening and morning but not the night, and a–"

"What did you just say?" Sean interrupts.

"What?"

"CCTV that places him in the town centre in the morning and evening but not the night."

"What time was the victim abducted?"

"10.23."

"Where from?"

"Outside Cheesy, a nightclub in the centre of town, but he'd already been seen getting on the bus at that time."

"That's it, August!"

Without any explanation, Sean bounces through the door and into the interrogation room. August can only stand perplexed as Sean immediately joins the questioning.

"You were caught on CCTV at 8.23, correct?" Sean asks,

interrupting Graham's questions. Graham is the master at interrogation, but even a master needs a bit of inspiration.

"No com—"

"Don't bloody no comment me you idiot, you are only confirming what you've already said, you can do that."

Despite appearing taken aback, the suspect turns to his lawyer, who nods gently.

"Yes," the suspect's croaky voice answers, his filthy jaw opening to reveal very few teeth.

"And you were seen getting on the bus at 8.55. One hour twenty-seven minutes before the abduction. Meaning there is no way you could have still been in town?"

"Yep."

Sean sifts through the CCTV images before him. He finds the image of the bus and presents it to the perpetrator.

"What number bus is that?"

"What?"

"Read the number."

"You can read the—"

"I said *read* the number."

The suspect peers forward slightly.

"Sixty-three," he grunts.

Sean takes out his phone and begins scrolling through something. An awkward silence settles upon the room, prompting the exchange of a few nervous looks.

"Excuse me, Detective," the lawyer pipes up, "But we are not here to go on our phones, and unless you—"

"Here it is," Sean declares. He places his phone on the table in front of the suspect, the screen revealing the bus timetable for bus number sixty-three.

"Where does the bus go?" Sean asks. "Going by what the timetable says."

"Look, I don't see why this—" the lawyer attempts.

"I weren't asking you."

The suspect looks to the lawyer who shrugs despondently, and the suspect, giving a look of pure exasperation, looks at the timetable on the phone.

"Back to Hester's Way. Where I live!"

"Yes. Yes, you do. And can you tell me what time the bus arrives in Hester's Way?"

"Er, it says 9.30."

Sean sifts through the CCTV images, finding an image taken by a traffic camera near Hester's Way at 9.32. Of the bus. With the suspect's inflated face peering out of the window.

"This is you on the bus at 9.32."

"So the bus was late. Big deal."

"No, this bus is not heading toward Hester's Way. It's already been there, and now it is heading away from Hester's Way. And if you could please just look at the timetable and tell me where the bus goes after Hester's Way."

The suspect looks then sits back.

"No comment," he says.

"For the record," Sean gleefully declares, speaking into the voice recorder. "The bus goes back into the town centre after Hester's Way. Which is where the bus is directed in this image."

The suspect and the lawyer look at each other like children caught passing notes in class.

"Now," Sean says, "Would you like to tell us what happened after you arrived back to town?"

August smiles. He can't help it.

That is the moment. The time and place where he realises he is witnessing the birth of one of the best detective minds he will ever meet.

He can not wait to see what becomes of this man.

Chapter Nineteen

Sean stands behind the one-way window to the interrogation room, watching Toby Marshall shivering beneath a blanket.

"They've done tests on the blood on his face," Elizabeth tells no one in particular. "It's not his. It's his wife's."

Sean nods.

Thinks.

August watches him.

Graham watches him.

Waiting.

Sean turns to Graham. The best interrogator they have, and one Sean has worked with many times in his career. The way this man uses words to coax suspects into their own traps is a work of art.

But Sean has his own instincts too.

"I'm going in," he tells them.

"But, Sean–" objects August.

Sean raises his hand.

"I'll leave it to Graham for the bulk, I just want a few minutes first."

August goes to protest again, but Sean stops him.

"You want my help, don't you?"

August looks to Graham as if waiting for his thoughts. Sean doesn't wait. He walks through the door, through the corridor and into the interrogation room, where he takes his seat opposite Toby.

Toby looks like all victims do. Sad. Grieving. Wounded.

Funny really, because that's often how villains look as well.

"Mr Marshall, I am Detective Inspector Sean Mallon. In a moment, my colleague Detective Constable Graham Shooter will be through to talk to you, but I just have a few questions first."

Toby vaguely nods, his eyes wide, staring with an intense absence. Probably from shock, possibly not.

"How many of you were in the room when Lois died?"

"Er…" he stutters.

"Take your time," Sean says reassuringly. He doesn't mean it.

"Three, I think, there were, er – three."

"You're sure?"

Toby nods. His mouth still hangs open like a dog, and his eyes stare at vacant corners of the room.

"Can you identify those that were there?"

"Well, there was me, my wife, and…"

"Yes?"

"The person who…"

He can't say it. Sean doesn't blame him. He nods. Allows him this weakness.

"You've not offered us much in description so far. You've told us their voice was disguised. Their face covered. What else can you tell us about the killer?"

Toby flinches at the word killer.

"I don't… I can't think…"

"Why did they choose you, Toby?"

"I… I don't…"

Sean huffs. Looks around. He doesn't have the patience for this.

"So you don't know why they chose you? What their motive was?"

He shakes his head gormlessly.

Sean leans forward.

"Tell me what the photos we found beside your wife were of."

"…Me…" he whimpers, tears accumulating in the corners of his eyes.

I don't buy it.

"Man up, Toby. You did something bad, and those images showed us that, right?"

"…right."

"Good, so now we're on the same page. Would you like to tell us more?"

Sean watches Toby for a few seconds. Fidgeting. Squirming. Unable to look Sean in the eye, staring at nothingness.

"I had an affair," he finally admits in a weak, distant voice that sounds like it's caught inside a tiny box.

"Okay, Toby, I'm going to put my cards on the table, want to hear them?"

Toby doesn't respond.

"Look me in the fucking eyes, Toby."

Sean knows August will be flinching, readying himself to burst in and stop any sign of the infamous Sean Mallon temper. Sean reminds himself to be careful how he uses his words. Patience isn't something he finds easy anymore.

Toby finally raises his head, holding weak eye contact with Sean, his eyes bloodshot and damp.

"You're not the first. You're not the second. Hell, I doubt you're even the last. But these crime scenes follow a very specific pattern. There is always a victim and a villain. Always redemption. You following?"

Toby forces a feeble nod.

"Good. So this 'redemption killer,' as we're calling them, got you and your wife because one is the villain, one is the victim, you understand?"

Toby nods.

"Crackin'. So why don't you tell us then, between you and your wife – who was the villain?"

His mouth opens but nothing comes out. It's as if he can't bring himself to admit it.

"Were you the villain, Toby? Were you?"

Toby closes his eyes and forces a small nod.

"Open your bloody eyes, I'm not having a conversation with your eyelids."

Toby forces them open.

"My question then, Toby, is this – you are the first out of each pairing where the villain isn't in the body bag. The villain always dies. Always. Until now. With you."

Sean's eyebrows narrow. He sees Toby realise that Sean has a point. That he has a question he's getting to.

"So why, Toby, are you the only villain to have survived, where the victim has not?"

Toby goes to open his mouth. Struggles. He has an answer ready, it's there on the tip of his tongue, waiting to be forced out.

"Yes?" Sean prompts.

"He told her to kill me. But she wouldn't."

"So who killed her then? The other person in the room?" Sean leans forward. "Or you?"

"What?"

"Be honest with me, Toby, I'll know if you're fucking with me."

"No!" Toby's eyes widen with terror. "I didn't touch her!"

Sean studies Toby. Studies his face. Watches. Soaks him up. Every red blemish, every inch of expression, every ill reaction.

Sean stands, leaves the room and re-joins August, where he watches Toby weep through the one-way window.

"He's not lying," Sean tells August, who stares at him, dumbfounded. He ignores August and turns to Graham. "He's all yours."

Sean turns to leave.

"Where are you going?" August asks.

"Home."

"But we're just getting started."

Sean looks to Toby, then back to August.

"We have nothing. You can question him all night, he's got nothing to give. You may as well wait for the next body, hope that one gives you more."

"The next body? Do you not care that the next body will be another dead victim?"

Sean stares numbly at August. "Anything else?"

"We have a load of forensic tests we need to look at, Sean, we need your eyes for them."

"I did what you asked. I gave my advice. Now I'm busy." Sean lifts his phone and smiles mischievously, displaying the name Carmen on the screen. "I'm going to be preoccupied."

"Carmen?" August responds. "Who's Carmen?"

Sean leaves before anyone can stop him.

He has a beautiful woman waiting for him at home, and no body or test will stop him from enjoying her.

Chapter Twenty

IT'S ALL COMING TOGETHER.

And that was the first time the victim had ever refused.

How exciting.

How terribly exciting!

Now for the next.

Then for the big finale.

And you aren't going to want to miss the big finale.

Elusive vs deviant.

Tricky vs clueless.

Light vs dark.

Villain vs villain.

Perfect.

I'm a God.

A messiah.

An artist.

Painting with the blood of the wronged.

And I can't wait to finish my masterpiece.

Chapter Twenty-One

CARMEN'S BODY CURVES PERFECTLY, A SET OF FAULTLESSLY connecting shapes coming together to form a work of art.

He feels her warm breasts pressed against his chest. He feels them rub along his scarred skin. It makes her purr.

His fingers dig into her back as she moves back and forth. She moans and he doesn't have any idea whether she's faking it or not and to be honest he does not care.

Being inside of her makes it all go away.

There is just them. Two bodies. Heat.

Nothing else.

He grabs her hair and she yelps but doesn't stop him. She licks her lips to show that she loves it, she loves it when he's rough, just as much as she loves it when he's tender.

When he finishes they stop and she stays on top of him. He is still inside of her, getting softer, but remaining encased in warmth.

She doesn't move. She is still. Her sweaty skin sticks to his, her dainty hands lost in his sweaty hair, her thighs pressed firmly against the outside of his legs, shaking, throbbing, in the way that a woman can't fake.

He looks her in the eyes.

She looks different. The way a person does when it's dark and they are lit by shadows. The amber glow of the street-light casts a sensual radiance over her face.

Her eyes seem bigger somehow. Her hair messier. Her skin faultless.

She is faultless.

She leans her head down and kisses him, softly, firmly, and moves so that he's no longer inside of her. She slumps to his side, lying next to him, facing him. Her hand rubs his scrotum, dragging upwards, tracing the marks on his chest. He puts an arm around her and pulls his other arm over her too. Her buttocks press against his crotch, her smooth back presses her spine against his torso. He looks down at her and kisses her collarbone, making her body flutter.

He closes his eyes. Leans his head against the back of hers. Smells her lavender shampoo and perspiration entangled together.

He runs his hand down her body. As he does, he comes across something on her hip. A scar. A wound from long ago.

"What's this?" Sean asks, whispering in her ear.

"It's a scar. I fell off my bike, fell on a sharp fence when I was a child. Cut me open."

"Wow, does it hurt?"

"If you apply pressure to it, it kills."

He nestles his head into the back of her neck, soaking himself in the smell of her sweat.

He feels her head move, and he opens his eyes to see why.

She is looking at the clock.

Why did she have to do that?

It shatters the illusion.

"How long can you stay?" he whispers, not wanting to ruin the moment with sound.

"About an hour," she tells him.

"But – I thought you were going to stay the night?"

"I can't today, I have another client."

And suddenly it's all meaningless.

The scraping of their skin. The closeness of her bare body. The gentle kisses of affection.

It means nothing.

Because another guy is going to get it in an hour.

But that look in her eye – the one she had when she kissed him as she rode him with passion and fever and intensity.

Was it all an act?

Does it matter?

She isn't running away. She is still lying there, in his arms. Pressing her naked body against his. Her perfect body against his scarred, bedraggled mess.

He pretends she isn't there because he pays her to be.

He pretends that she loves him.

It feels good for as long as the delusion lasts. Then he realises he is holding something that will never be his. Something temporary. Something… lost.

And once again he feels alone. Like he did before, and like he does now.

He wonders if she is like this with other clients.

Close. Spooning. Softly kissing.

Is it just part of her job to make him feel this way, or is there something special about him?

He wonders if she ever talks about him to anyone else.

Whether she refers to him as a client.

And again, he realises, it doesn't matter.

Why would she think there was something special about him?

There isn't.

It's a service.

No one ever does an MOT on his banged-up perishing car then decides they want to keep it.

No barman ever tells his other punters about the alcoholic loser who bums around his pub.

Still, he wishes it was different. He make-believes it is. Pretends they are getting married. Having a baby. She'll drive him to AA meetings, smile at him in the morning, and giggle as he kisses her freckles.

Her eyes are so blameless. So lost.

He wishes he could protect her.

She looks too innocent to be a whore.

No.

Don't call her that.

He would never let anyone call her that. She is not a whore.

She is…

Mine.

No.

"Have you ever thought," Sean muses in the husky, croaky voice he gets after a whole day spent drinking whiskey. "I mean, ever considered…"

"Considered what, baby?"

The way she calls him baby makes him melt. Makes him feel like he's hers.

"I don't know. What life would be like if I weren't a client?"

"You don't want to see me anymore?"

"No, no – not at all. I mean, if I weren't a client. If I were… a boyfriend."

She laughs. Giggles and laughs at him. At the ridiculous nature of his suggestion. Because he's joking. Of course, he is. Why wouldn't he be?

"You pay me to be your fantasy. That's all I am."

"No, you are so much more."

"Take away the moments we spend together, and think about it – would you really be happy picking wallpaper with me? Talking to me about the weather across the breakfast table? Sorting out our finances?"

He understands what she's saying, but still, the thought of doing such things with her fills him with happiness and pride.

"I like a lot of money," she says. "Would you have enough to keep me?"

He closes his eyes. Bows his head. Dreams.

"What if you were to just, I don't know – run away with me? We'd rob a bank or something. I know enough about the criminal world that I know how to get away with it. We could live on our millions."

She laughs again.

"You're so funny, Sean."

Now that hurts.

Pierces his broken gut with a thousand sharp knives. Punches through him, into him, cutting him deep.

His heart collapses into a soggy mess.

"You can go now," he tells her as he stands and walks into the bathroom. His crotch feels sticky and he wants a shower.

"But Sean, I don't need to go until–"

"Money's in the drawer," he tells her as he slams the bathroom door behind him.

Chapter Twenty-Two

Jade looks to her side.

She checks no one is watching her.

Because that's how she wants to be. Unnoticed. Alone. Never interacted with.

This is the first time she's been out of her house in two years and she is terrified.

Everyone looks evil. Everyone looks like a villain, or an assailant, who could just jump out at her, punch her, wielding a knife against her.

A group of youths laugh. Two blokes argue. A woman shouts at her dog.

All of them. Any of them.

They could hurt her.

Obsessive Compulsive Disorder they called it. Post-Traumatic Stress Disorder from someone else. Agrophobia was the last that she heard.

It is none of the above.

It's fear.

The last time she was out alone it happened. In a crowded Saturday afternoon in a busy town centre. She was walking across Montpellier, what's supposed to be the expensive high street of Cheltenham. Minding her own business. Thinking about a date she had that night, wondering if she had time for a bath, holding her purchases securely in a plastic bag by her side – she used to love the feeling of carrying a plastic bag full of clothes she had just bought; it's something she felt in childhood and never went away.

He came up behind her.

Called her a slag.

Punched her in the back of the head.

Took her purse. Her bags. God knows what he wanted with a new dress, but he took it anyway.

Then his friends came in. Kicked her in the ribs. Blackened her eyes. Humiliated her.

Then ran off.

No one did anything.

A busy Saturday afternoon in a town centre and no one did a damn thing.

They walked past. Protected themselves. Hoping that if they didn't intervene, then they would be spared the hurt she had just suffered.

She lay on the floor, nursing her injuries.

People hustling and bustling past her.

One teenager even tripped over her.

That was the scariest part.

Not that she was attacked, but that hundreds of people walked past as she lay helplessly sobbing on the floor and did nothing.

She had to quit her job. She couldn't go.

The house became her sanctity.

To leave it was to face mortifying dread.

They had robbed her of more than just a dress. They had robbed her of her liberty. Of being able to escape the four walls of her abode.

Now here she stands.

Many sessions of expensive at-home therapy later.

She can't go down Montpellier Road. She can't. She can't face that street yet. Baby steps. She knows it's irrational, to think it would happen in the exact same place, but just looking down that street fills her with dread, and she can't do it, she cannot do it.

So she walks down the high street. Past WHSmith's where she used to spend ages finding the right magazine, never paying attention to anyone around her.

Now she takes in every bit of her surroundings.

She looks around constantly, aware of everyone and everything. A mother and child walk past, the mother scalding the child in the midst of a tantrum. A couple comes up behind her, arms around each other, eternally in love. A guy in a tracksuit walks toward her, a face full of anger, and she crosses the road to avoid him.

She is shaking. Her arms are going like a washing machine. Sweating. Vibrating. She can't stand still. She shifts her weight from one leg to the other.

Why is she doing this?

Why did she convince herself she could?

The police couldn't identify them on CCTV. They said it wasn't enough. They couldn't see their faces.

They could still be here.

Stop it.

Stop it, for God's sake.

What, they are just going to be waiting around after two years for her to venture into town?

I'm being ridiculous.

She looks up. Takes a big breath.

Everyone looks annoyed.

Everyone keeps staring.

Every face is the face of an attacker, someone who could

find the motivation to come at her, to hurt her, to find some way to—

No.

I'm stronger than this.

She considers that statement.

But am I?

Would someone who is strong let someone force them into the confines of a house for two years?

Two years.

It's probably longer than they would get in prison.

She looks to her feet. Wills them to shuffle forward. Someone bumps into her and curses her under their breath.

Her body tenses, waiting for their retaliation.

But they don't.

They just hastily fade into the distance.

She's fine.

Absolutely fine.

She starts to relax.

Time to grow up. Time to get my life back.

She stands up straight and walks forward. She smiles.

I can do this.

That's when they get her.

Chapter Twenty-Three

SEAN ENTERS THE POLICE STATION AND, ALMOST AS IF SHE'D been waiting for him, Elizabeth appears, grabbing his arm and dragging him forward.

"We have something!" she claims.

"You found something?" Sean exclaims. "A sighting of Victor?"

"No, Sean," Elizabeth reluctantly answers. She leads him through the station via a different route than he would normally go. He enters a new murder incident room, finding an image printed from CCTV in the town centre.

Sean sighs. Realises that this has nothing to do with Victor.

"Toby Marshall described the suspect as having a long black jacket with a hood up," she tells him, speaking at a million miles per hour.

Sean rubs his head, trying to get rid of his groggy state.

"We have CCTV images of someone matching description abducting someone in the town centre."

Sean surveys the board, tracing his eyes over a series of

CCTV images. He brushes his greasy hair out of his eyes, shakes his head in an attempt to break out of his tired mind, and studies them. The first is of a young woman standing in town, oddly still. The next shows the attacker in a hood behind them.

The next image shows the attacker bludgeoning the woman over the head.

The next shows the woman being dragged.

"Identified the weapon?" he asks.

"We're thinking a hammer or piece of wood or similar. It's too out of focus when we zoom in."

Too out of focus?

In a society where people have high-definition cameras on their phones, it is too out of focus?

Ridiculous.

Sean scans the next screenshot of the suspect lifting the victim into the boot of a car, and the next where the car is driving away.

At least the license plate was in focus.

"Have we tracked the car on the traffic cams?"

"Yes, we're just waiting on a location."

Sean nods.

This feels strange.

Wrong, somehow.

"I don't get it," Sean thinks aloud.

"Don't get what?"

"Why would they do this in an open town centre? It seems sloppy."

"They messed up."

"No, they have numerous victims without messing up so far, why mess up now? Surely they know their car is in plain sight of CCTV, they will know we can follow them."

"Maybe they don't."

"No, to get away with four already, leaving us such little

evidence – they know what they are doing. This means they want to be caught."

Elizabeth pulls a face of confusion.

"Why would they want to be caught?"

Sean turns to her with a sting of pride.

"That, Elizabeth, is the million-dollar question."

August bursts into the room waving a piece of paper in the air.

"We have an address people, let's go!" he announces.

The whole room jumps into action. Elizabeth disappears with a group of other officers and August arrives at Sean's side.

"You ride with me, Sean," August instructs.

Sean absently follows.

Bemused. Confused. Rattled.

This just doesn't add up.

He tries to convince himself he's being jaded. That he's failed so many times at capturing Victor Crane, and it's taken its toll on his cynicism.

But no.

That's not it.

It just feels like this is all part of the killer's plan.

Dear Sean,

Oh, what a lovely day it is!

I'm on holiday, Sean, and the sun is shining, and I am basking in it. On a beach with sunshine, and lots of children happily making sand castles.

Obviously, I can't divulge where in particular I am, but I am having a ball. Seagulls screeching, skin tanning, children laughing.

Did I mention the children laughing?

It's good to see that you are occupying your mind with things other than me. It's what we agreed. And I think it will do you a world of good.

Honestly, why waste time on me?

I'm a lost cause.

There are plenty of murderers out there who aren't as slippery as I am, who can't evade police capture as expertly as I have. Surely your time is better spent chasing them. You may actually have a chance.

It is a lovely day, Sean.

I wish you were here.

I'd buy you an ice cream. Not a beer – you've had enough of those. But maybe some fish and chips on the beach. But not beer.

Because it will destroy your liver and you'll be dead within years!

And where would the fun in that be?

I don't want you to die. Why would I? You're my favourite pastime.

So. Let's talk business.

The Redemption Killer.

This killer is a fascinating specimen. But foolish. They will mess up. Stay with it, Sean, you will get them.

Still, I can't help but admire their artistry. They know how to set up a crime scene. But they make their motive too clear, too easy for me. I think a true artist will make you do a little bit of the work. Personally, I find this whole victim and villain thing to be just a little too obvious.

But the way they set up the crime scene for your arrival is beautiful.

I always took pride in how I left my bodies for discovery. Pictured your face as you gagged. I'd love to have seen you as you discovered them but, alas, to remain uncaught I was never really able to stick around. I'm better than that.

But The Redemption Killer isn't.

Stick at it, Sean, you are on the right track.

I miss you and hope to see you again someday.

Until then.

Your friend,

Victor Crane

Chapter Twenty-Four

A BUCKET OF FREEZING WATER WAKES JADE FROM HER unconscious state. She shakes it off, brushes the water from her eyes, wipes them on her sleeve.

She is freezing. Shaking.

She goes to stand.

She can't.

She looks down.

Her feet are fastened to a chair. She checks the rest of her body, which is free.

On her lap. A knife. In her hand.

She looks up. She can't tell where she is.

"You are a victim, Jade," a voice tells her. It's disguised, like it's through one of those voice changers. She turns around and sees someone standing behind her with a hood over their head. She can't see their face, it's in shadow, but they are smaller than the sinister voice suggests.

"Who are you?" she asks.

"A friend," they reply.

Jade looks in front of her.

A man sits opposite. Staring at her. Wide eyes. Terrified

eyes. The rope around his chest, restraints around his ankles, duct tape around his mouth. He looks desperate. He cries. His head keeps shaking, he tries to say something, but it just comes through as muffles.

He won't stop staring at her.

The whole time, he stares at her. Not at the person over her shoulder, but at Jade. As if he recognises her. As if it's the sight of her that's scaring him – not the person behind her, not the restraints that stop him from being able to move, but her.

Like he's seen a ghost.

There's something about her that puts the fear of God into him.

"I didn't do this," she tells him, wondering if that's why he's looking at her like this, thinking it's her that set them up.

"He knows," the voice tells her.

She turns around and stares at the person lurking in the shadows.

They stand in front of a whiteboard.

It's a classroom. In a school.

The blinds are down, thin cracks spreading narrow shafts of light over childish displays. She deduces it's a primary school based on the size of the chairs and the posters about phonetics on the walls.

Why here?

Then she realises.

This was her classroom. When she was a teacher. Before she had to quit her job because she was too scared to leave the house. Before she had to give up everything.

Except, those aren't her displays. The tables have been rearranged. The teacher's desk faces a different way.

The man is still staring at her. His eyebrows lift, his alert eyes moving from her face to the knife to her face to the knife.

"Why am I here?" she asks, hearing the quiver in her voice.

"You don't need to worry, Jade. I'm not here to hurt you. *He* is the one who needs to worry."

She looks at the man staring back at her.

For some reason, she doesn't fear the person stood behind her. She fears this man tied up. But she doesn't know why.

His face is distantly familiar.

"You are a victim," the voice continues. "You were left helpless. Stuck at your parent's home. Living off them as a grown adult."

"I – I don't understand. What does this have to do with–"

She's holding a knife.

She becomes suddenly aware that she is holding a knife.

This man's face begins to fade into the realms of recognition.

"This man in front of you. You know him."

"I – I don't."

"His name is Ian Holdsworth."

As if a name she doesn't know prompts a memory from the back of her mind, she realises.

She knows who this man is.

The delinquent, sinister, unquantifiable prick. The bastard. The miscreant arsehole.

Any thought of fear perishes out of her, taken over by rage. She doesn't care about anything anymore. Anger bursts against the constraints of her skin, surging through her like water through a collapsing dam.

No wonder he looks back at her with eyes so terrified.

He should be terrified.

He knows what he's done to her. He knows what she's suffered, the conditions she's found herself in, the days and days and days spent indoors, shaking in fear that the doorbell might ring.

All because of him.

"I am giving you the option to–"

She doesn't need to hear the option.

She lunges forward and sticks the knife into his throat and retracts it. She watches as blood sprays like a leaky barrel. He gasps for oxygen that doesn't come. Blood gushes down his restraints, drenching his filthy body.

She takes off his gag.

She smirks. He screams. He shouts. But it all turns into croaky moans as he loses the ability to speak.

She hears sirens in the distance.

The man's body grows limp.

What have I done?

Chapter Twenty-Five

SEAN LAUNCHES HIMSELF UP THE STEPS THREE AT A TIME. He's out of breath before he's barely begun, but he perseveres, determined to do something right for once.

August and Elizabeth follow behind, trailed by more constables.

They were worried they wouldn't know where to go when they got to the school, but there was one classroom with one light on.

This only confirmed Sean's fears that this was all part of the plan.

Only an idiot would make such a huge slip up unintentionally.

Still, Sean was keen to see what the killer wanted them to find. If there was a possibility of saving a life, they had to take it.

He pants. Ignores his stitch. Forces himself upwards. Trying with everything he has.

He kicks open a set of double doors and sprints down the corridor, searching for the classroom with a light on.

At the end of the long corridor, a door opens.

A figure emerges.

So far away.

He runs. Reaches out. Nearly there.

But the figure is distant. Unattainable.

Their face is disguised by a hood. Small. Evidently agile. They look at him. Eyes disguised, but Sean can feel them, burning him.

They exit through a door behind them.

Sean runs. Sprints. Charges forward, battling against aching thighs and breath that won't catch up.

He reaches the open door to the classroom. Two bodies are in it, both covered in blood, but it doesn't slow him down.

"August!" he prompts over his shoulder.

"Got it!" August confirms. Priority is always the preservation of life, and he will see to that.

Sean continues running.

Elizabeth stays with him.

She's young. She has good legs, an athletic build. Her breathing isn't even heavy, she barely sweats. Sean can already feel his shirt growing heavy beneath his armpits.

He kicks his way through another set of doors. Halts next to stairs leading both upwards and downwards.

He sees them.

Descending. Already two, nearly three floors down.

Sean jumps down the first five steps, turns the corner and does the same with the next five steps. Elizabeth takes them one at a time but keeps Sean's pace.

His body suffers. He wants to stop. To catch a breath. Perspiration sticks his shirt to him, his heart pumping so fast he fears he may go into cardiac arrest at any moment.

The killer reaches the bottom floor and disappears.

The temptation to quit is great. Let Elizabeth go on. She's quick. He'll catch up when he can.

But no.

This is his chance.

He pretends its Victor Crane, and as soon as he does that, nothing will stop him.

He pushes forward. Elizabeth loyally at his side, keeping stride.

He reaches the bottom floor. There's only one pair of doors he can enter, so he barges through them shoulder-first. They sprint down the corridor, no sight of the suspect before them, but knowing this must be the right direction. They make it into the cafeteria, which is a big open space with many doors, but they instinctively drive toward the exit.

Sean picks up his radio.

"This is Mallon," he manages between heavy breaths. "In pursuit," pant, "of subject," pant, "heading through cafeteria," pant, "aiming at south exit," pant, "over."

He barges through the fire exit with such force that the heavy door rebounds against his face and hits his nose. He recoils like he's been punched but doesn't dwell on it. He perseveres, as does Elizabeth.

He sees officers running toward the exit, but they are too far away.

He stops. Scans the area.

In the distance, across multiple football pitches, Sean sees the suspect leap over a far bush.

Even though they know it's futile, even though they know there is no police presence there, and multiple places the suspect can go, they still try, still keep going, this time with the dozen police officers who had appeared for support at the south exit behind them.

The open field feels so long. The bush in the distance looks so far away. No matter how much he runs, it doesn't get closer.

He looks to Elizabeth, sprinting like a robot, no fading of her resolve, no hesitance, no perspiration.

They reach the bush and Elizabeth jumps over it with ease.

Sean tries but collapses. He grabs hold of a few branches that prick his hands, rolls and lands in a lump on the floor, stinging from various twigs dug into his increasingly painful stitch.

Fuck me, I'm an embarrassment.

He pushes himself to his feet and stumbles forward. He can see Elizabeth running down a side path and assumes she is running that way for a reason, so follows, soldiering forward, pushing himself.

But it's not enough.

He can feel himself lagging.

As much as he wants to accelerate, his legs just won't. They feel heavy. Like he's wading through water. Like weights are attached to his ankles.

The other police officers progress past him, overtaking him.

He almost trips over his own feet as he barges through an alleyway. He uses the wall to propel himself forward but just finds himself slowing down.

Jesus Christ, I'm going to collapse.

He drags himself to the end of the alleyway, now out of sight of any officer. He comes to a roundabout. It's busy. He looks to his left, then his right.

There stands Elizabeth, along with the rest of the officers. Bending over, catching her breath.

He looks at her with expectancy, denial disguised as optimism.

She shakes her head.

His fists ball. Tight. Ready to punch something.

He falls onto his back, his breath still racing ahead of him. The sky spins in circles, clouds rushing past. Dizziness takes over his mind. It's at least ten minutes until his breathing calms down.

That's when he realises they are all looking at him.

For him to make the call. Give them an instruction. Tell them what to do next.

He doesn't know what to say.

His fists clench harder. He closes his eyes. Wills himself to control his temper, but willpower is not enough, and he kicks a nearby cone then punches the brick wall.

"*Fuck!*" he screams so hard his lungs blister until he feels the hurt, feels every bit of his chest wheezing with pain from the strain on his voice.

If only he wasn't a shitty alcoholic.

He'd have had them a few years ago. Would have caught up without a problem.

I'm nothing now.

"Get a roadblock for each direction," Sean demands of the nearest officer as his senses begin to return.

The officer gets onto his radio and hastily issues instructions.

"It's okay, there's nothing we could have done," Elizabeth tells him.

"Oh, fuck off," he replies.

Now's not the time.

Chapter Twenty-Six

August has the room sealed off and the scene of the crime officers working efficiently.

Jade Conway is sat with a nearby officer with her hands restrained behind her back. It isn't long before her bloody hands are matched with the only handprints on the knife used to kill the man slumped dead in the other chair. Though he knows it can't be as simple as that, August still gives the go-ahead for his team to make the arrest and take her to the station.

He oversees the classroom next door as a temporary incident room to collate and register evidence. August makes contact with the headmaster of the school and finds him to be very accommodating, receiving promises that the school will help in any way they can.

Sean walks into this incident room, stumbling from desk to desk. His face is red. August can smell the stale alcohol on his clothes mixing with body odour.

"Did you get them?" he asks, but he already knows the answer.

This is confirmed when Elizabeth follows Sean into the

room, shaking her head.

Sean kicks off. Throwing chairs, ripping apart exercise books, punching the whiteboard. Providing the typical Sean Mallon Temper Tantrum Show that, in all honesty, no one reacts to because they are so bored of it.

When Sean goes to throw a bag of evidence, August intervenes, putting his hand on Sean's wrist to stop him.

"August, get your soddin' hands off me," Sean says.

"I think you need to go home, Sean."

"Go to hell, August, you wanted me here."

"Yes, and now I'm telling you that I don't want you here. Go home."

Sean looks to August with a mixture of furious retaliation and dented pride as if he was just emasculated before the entire department. August can see the argument brewing in Sean's face, and truly does not want to bite.

Sean shoves August.

He takes it.

"Go home, Sean," August repeats, keeping his voice emotionless, monotone, direct, refusing to allow his feelings to enter this. He can't. He has to be better than that.

"Fuck you, August."

Sean shoves him again.

"Sean, go home."

Sean shakes his head, goes to shove August again, but August grabs his arms.

He stares intently into Sean's eyes. Holding him still. Willing him to cooperate.

Sean finally gets the message.

He leaves, stumbling against the wall.

"See him out," August tells the nearest officer, glad he's doing that job rather than August.

"August, if I may," comes Elizabeth's voice nearby.

"What?" August says, then feels bad for sounding so irritable. It's not her fault.

"What is it?" August tries again, attempting to sound calm.

"Can I just ask – why is he here?"

August sighs. That's a good question.

"He was brilliant," she says. "But when he was sober."

"That brilliance is still there, he just…" August trails off, unsure how to finish that sentence, finding it more and more difficult to justify Sean's reckless actions.

"I'm sorry, but it's not. It was once, but now, he's barely a shell of who he was."

"Put yourself in his position. His daughter was paralysed because of him and his job."

"Yes, but that's not my fault," she insists. "Nor is it the victim's fault. Or your fault. They all deserve better."

August rubs his sinus.

He knows she's right. But she's… new. She doesn't understand. She didn't know the Sean Mallon before. The Sean Mallon that earned his legendary status.

"Just… trust me," he tells her.

"But, if it's not out of line, he is a liability who–"

"It is out of line," August snaps, growing tired of this argument.

Growing tired of having nothing left to say when it comes to justifying Sean's presence and job title.

"I apologise," she says. "I'll get back to work."

"Thank you," August says softly, showing his appreciation.

He leans back against the desk.

Watches everyone work in front of him.

Wondering what difference Sean has actually made to this operation. What help bringing him on board was.

She's right. He knows it. But he can't admit it.

He's got brilliance in him, he just...

He lost it, I guess.

August knows he needs to make a decision: Whether or not he's prepared to continue picking up the slack when Sean continues to let him down.

Chapter Twenty-Seven

SEAN KNOWS JACK CAN TELL HE'S DRUNK. HE'S TRYING TO stay on his seat, trying not to slur his words or hiccup.

But he sees the look of disgrace that Jack wears.

Hypocritical, really.

He hiccups.

Because Jack – well, he – he did bad stuff – so how can he – *hic – start looking at me like I'm the piece of shit.*

He's the piece of shit.

Sean drinks his tea. Dribbles it down his chin. Feels it run down his neck and down his collar and *damn* that's another shirt that's stained and will have to be thrown out.

He could try washing it, but – effort, you know?

"What are you doing, Sean?" Jack asks. He hasn't touched his cup of tea and Mars bar.

Blah blah blah.

Another person taking the role of my mother.

Beat the crap out of him, tell him he's worthless, that they're his mother. Then there'll be his father. Or then they… or… he… *what?*

"What-a-you-meaning?" Sean asks, feeling each word meld into one.

"You're pathetic," Jack says. "You're pissed out your face. I'm surprised they even let you in."

"Let me in? Course they let me in! They all let me in, 'cause, I tell you, 'cause – 'cause I'm Sean Mallon."

Jack shakes his head. Runs his fingers over the side of his mug. Still doesn't drink it.

Sean goes to drink his, then remembers he stained his collar and decides not to, so puts it down too hard and it splashes over the table so he uses his shirt cuff to wipe it and *there's another bloody stain now!*

"Sean Mallon," Jack repeats in a mocking tone. "Yes, of course, you are Sean Mallon."

"Who are you to talk, you – you murderous peedfile!" He forgets how to say paedophile.

Jack leans toward Sean.

"Then why do you come?" he asks with a shrug of his shoulders.

"What?"

"Then why do you come here? Why do you visit me?"

"I…"

"Victor Crane and I are equally guilty for what happened to your daughter. Yet you hunt *him*, then sit and make small talk with *me*. As if we're friends. As if none of it ever actually happened. Why?"

Sean stutters, struggling for an answer.

"I'll tell you," Jack continues. "It's because you're lonely. And you have no one else."

"Not true."

"You're a disgrace. You're embarrassing me, and I'm in prison. I'm stuck here for life, and *you* are embarrassing *me.*"

"Whatever, man…"

"Seriously, what are we doing here? Are you so fucking

bored that you have to visit the guy who abducted you and tried to kill you? Am I the only person you can find to give you the time of day?"

Sean's head is heavy. He drops it. Lets it dangle, loll, as he rubs his neck.

"I killed people, Sean. I helped kidnap your daughter."

"Yes, but I killed Alexander Shirlov in cold blood, you had reasons."

"Alexander Shirlov was a murderer. I hurt your daughter, someone innocent."

"No, Victor hurt my daughter."

"You are deluded, Sean."

"Shut up."

He's had enough. He tries covering his ears, but he hears everything.

"We are not friends," Jack persists. "We never have been friends. I'm just someone you visit so you don't have to be stuck with your own company for an extended period of time."

The bastard.

The prick.

How dare he?

I come to visit him, and he– he–

How dare he!

Who does he think he is?

Sean dives across the table, knocking everything off, mugs smashing on the floor, chairs overturned. He places his hands around Jack's throat and takes him to the floor.

He squeezes.

Hard, then harder still. Watches as Jack's eyes bulge, as they stare helplessly back.

Jack's hands grip around Sean's wrists but make no effort to remove them. He lets them stay there. Allows himself to suffocate.

As if he deserves it.

As if he wants it.

Sean doesn't know what infuriates him more. Jack's words or his refusal to fight back.

"Fight back!" Sean demands. "Fight back!"

Jack doesn't.

He just looks up with his empty eyes, as if he wants this.

Sean is swept into the air. He looks around. Two prison officers have hold of him. He kicks his feet.

"Get the fuck off me!"

They drag him kicking and screaming through the hall and toward the exit. He thrashes his legs out, wriggles his arms, even tries throwing his head toward them in a headbutt that would no doubt hurt him more than it would hurt them.

It's no good.

The world is spinning. He's dizzy. Drowsy. Disgraced.

No one even bothers arresting him.

The next time he finds solid ground he's out of the prison and on the cold, wet floor of the car park. His palms sting as they land in the bumpy cement. His knees are wet in a puddle.

He looks at his hands.

Red, sore, bloody.

What am I doing?

He takes out his phone. Tries contacting Carmen. He doesn't know why, he just wants to talk to her.

It rings and rings and rings.

No answer.

The person he pays to give him company doesn't even want to give him company anymore.

I guess I pissed her off too.

Kneeling there, he realises, for the first time in a long, long time: he is alone.

Completely and utterly alone.

His only purpose evades him. He considers ending it all.

Right here, right now.

He could get rope from a DIY store on the way home. Pills from a pharmacist. A knife from the supermarket.

He shakes his head.

He knows he won't.

He doesn't even have the guts to do it.

He drags himself to his feet. Looks down at the ripped knees of his suit trousers.

His head is pounding so hard he worries that it may burst his skull.

He trudges through the country road and into the dark streets of the town, hoping someone would jump out and kill him.

Dear Sean,

Thank you for ceasing your operation and your hopeless endeavour to find me. It was wise, and I can see you are working hard on a new case.

As such, this will be the last letter I send you.

I feel that our time is up, and it's best that we both move on.

I will miss you and your friendship, which has always given me great comfort through the years. I will miss those phone calls we used to have, these letters I send to you. But, most of all, I will miss watching you uselessly try to find me whilst I'm barely metres away.

I know you visit Jack, and I think that's honourable, but if I may be so bold as to offer you some advice, then I would like to suggest that you left him alone too.

It's about time that we all moved on. Left this alone.

After all, that's the one thing you are in this world, isn't it?

Alone.

Just imagine what your life would be like if you gave all of this up. You could actually live it! You could make an honest living, give up the drink and settle down. Surround yourself with a family. A beautiful wife, a mortgage, a house of adoring kids, brothers, sisters, aunts, uncles, friends.

It is all so easily in your grasp, and you could have it. But I don't think you will let yourself. You know why, Sean?

Because you could be in a room with a hundred people you love and you would still be alone

It will never be good enough without a purpose. Something to make your life mean something.

To you, a life without purpose is a life unfulfilled.

But family could be your purpose. Love. Affection. Joy. Raising a group of adoring children. Doing an honest day's work. These are just as good purposes as anything. And, what's more, none of those purposes will kill you.

Don't convince yourself that you will one day find me, and that you would actually be happy if you did, or that you would even be content should you get your wife and daughter back.

I just don't think you're capable of it. But you could still try. You still have time.

Then again, I wouldn't be capable of it either.

That's where we are similar, Sean. We both persevere in our fight for a purpose. The only difference is that the purpose we see for ourselves is so very different from the other's.

My thoughts will always be with you.

Take care of yourself.

Your friend,

Victor Crane

Chapter Twenty-Eight

A FRANTIC RUSTLING ECHOES FROM A NEARBY ALLEY.

It's pitch black on the street, but further along the road, Sean can see a flickering lamp, lighting pasty white skin that moves back and forth in the depths of a backstreet.

Two lovers are going at it relentlessly.

He could arrest them for it. He could legitimately get them done for indecency. He could march them to the station, and he would be in full right, and they would be charged.

But what would be the point?

Just let them be happy.

Something he can't have.

No one ever really wants to be happy in this world, or so Sean convinces himself.

Happiness is an illusion.

A gift we never receive. Something we see before us, in the distance, something we work toward, reach our hands out to grasp, but then there's always another thing we have to do, something else that just makes this idea a mirage. An illusion. Hallucinations of a tired, determined mind.

Footsteps patter behind him.

They speed up.

The street is otherwise empty.

The footsteps stop.

He turns. Looks over his shoulder. There's no one there.

He walks again.

He hears them.

Someone is following him.

Good.

Let them kill me.

"Sean."

Upon hearing his name ever so faintly, Sean turns himself around and awaits a further explanation of who it is.

That's when something hard smashes into his forehead.

He stumbles for a moment, his vision growing blurry, and falls helplessly onto his back.

As the face of the killer beams back down at him, he feels his thoughts fade away.

His head drops.

His eyes close.

He doesn't know what happens after that.

Villain Vs Villain

Chapter Twenty-Nine

ANOTHER NASTY HANGOVER PULSATES AGAINST HIS CRANIUM and Sean regrets everything.

Flashes of memory return to him. The scenes he made, the things he said, the way he stumbled through the streets. He considers himself pathetic. Wishes he wasn't like this.

His dry throat gags for water.

He goes to get up, to leave his bed in search of food and drink.

But he can't.

Something is stopping him.

He goes to rub his eyes, but he can't.

His eyes adjust.

He's not at home.

It's pitch black. He can't see a thing. There's someone else there, as he can hear them breathing, heavily exhaling, like it's deliberate, like they want to be heard.

They say nothing.

They are alone in the disrupted silence.

Their breathing is so loud.

Bristles of rope burn against his arms as he tries to move.

Metal bumps against his restrained wrists. His legs are secured to the chair legs.

He's caught. Bound. Helpless. And his captor is in there with him.

"Hello?" he offers.

No one answers.

He tries to figure out how he got there. Who could have taken him?

Victor Crane?

No. It can't be. The letter said it was over. Victor may be a sick man, but he is true to his word.

Who then?

The Redemption Killer?

In which case, he's either the villain or the victim.

He can't move. The villain was the one who could never move.

Which tells him that somebody is going to be given the option of killing him.

Who?

Who could be the victim?

Form a queue...

The number of candidates wouldn't be a short list, what with the number of people he's verbally abused, badgered, bullied, pushed around. He is a complete and utter dick to everyone he meets.

He keeps himself calm.

He's been in this position before. He knows panicking doesn't help. He needs to be relaxed.

His breathing doesn't accelerate, his heartbeat doesn't quicken, and his fists do not clench. He's trained for these situations. He's experienced. He knows how to retain an air of dignified stillness that he can use to figure out what to do next.

Then again, isn't he grateful?

Grateful that this could be it? That he will be granted death?

Footsteps grow closer. The killer is here. The victim, the villain, the killer, all in the same room.

He listens carefully, sees if there are any clues as to where they are. Dripping, shouting, car engines – anything. But nothing gives it away.

So he keeps listening.

It takes five steps for the killer to arrive by his side, which means the door must be close. They are coming from behind his right shoulder. Their steps are hollow, like heels, and he can taste a lick of perfume as they stand beside him.

Perfume? Heels?

Is this a woman?

A transvestite?

A trick?

"Who are you?" Sean asks. Not that he imagines the killer would suddenly divulge their name, he just needs to establish contact, start a dialogue.

A low chuckle hits his ears.

They take a few steps further away and stop. Fiddle with something.

A light turns on.

Sean squints from the brightness, turning his face away. He allows a narrow lift of his eyelids, granting permission to a small seep of light to start the process of allowing his vision to adjust.

He rotates his head, tries to peer behind him, to see the killer, see what they look like. He can't turn his head enough.

"Who are you?" he tries again. "My name is Sean, what's yours?"

A typical negotiating tactic he'd used many times – first name basis creates more emotional connections. Names destroy anonymity.

Failing to see the killer, he turns to his other captor.

Strangely, they are tied up in the same way as him. As if they were also a villain.

As if they were both villains.

It doesn't make sense.

Then he lifts his head. Looks to see who they are.

That calmness he'd achieved fades. His whole body tenses. Fills with rage. Fills with anger, hostility, a desperation to lunge out from beneath his restraints, and attack the smug face before him.

The smug face of Victor Crane.

Chapter Thirty

WATCHING THE ORGANISED COMMOTION OF THE INCIDENT room makes August feel oddly proud, if only a little bit useless. Various stations are set up with various police officers working on various tasks. Some review CCTV files, some do victim profiling, some organise information on the board, some chase witnesses, some try to find the victims that got away – everyone has a job.

Except for August. Or so it feels. As his job is to run the operation. To make the tough calls.

He's been able to keep the media on a tense leash so far, but he knows that it won't be long before they realise how consistently useless this station is becoming.

They'll be after his job next.

He takes out his phone. Finds Sean's number.

The guy's a disgrace.

But he's the only one with this innate ability, that seems magic at times, to spot the very specific particulars that help you track a killer. Perhaps because his mind is equally deranged.

August knows that person is still in there. Once the

alcohol is taken away, and the self-loathing, and the self-pity – there is still that incredible mind beneath it. And that's the mind they need.

If only he'd answer his damn phone.

August tries him again. This is probably the first time Sean hasn't answered his phone. However drunken or perilous his state, he would answer. This job is his life. And he knows that any call could be the one about Victor Crane.

Even when asleep, Sean's mind is so in-tuned to the sound of his mobile phone ringing that it will stir him within seconds.

But this time he doesn't answer. It prompts a bad feeling to bulge the pit of August's stomach.

He becomes momentarily distracted. Elizabeth is playing a video on her monitor. A screen from the school. The hooded figure runs through, head down, giving nothing away.

Except…

"Elizabeth, stop it there," he instructs.

She pauses the video.

"Now rewind, frame by frame."

She does so.

The figure moves fractionally backwards on each static image. Completely covered. Adorned in black. All apart from their hands. Their hands, masked by fingerless gloves.

"Zoom in on those hands."

Elizabeth does so. She zooms in far enough that the blurry hand of the suspect fills the screen.

It starts to dawn on August.

The ridiculous assumptions one makes, even an experienced veteran like himself.

"Can you get rid of the pixilation?"

Elizabeth hits the button a few times and the image mildly restores.

The hand comes into focus.

The nails come into focus.

As does the nail polish.

"It's a woman," August muses.

Elizabeth turns and sees that something else is bothering him.

"What is it?"

"Sean's not answering his phone."

"So?"

August folds his arms. Stands up straight. Thinks.

Sean would always answer.

What could have happened to him?

Could he be being targeted?

A ridiculous idea, he knew that, but – like Sean said, the whole situation at the school seemed too deliberate, too set up; could it have been for Sean's benefit?

"Surely he's just drunk or asleep somewhere?" Elizabeth points out.

"No," August defies her. "No matter how drunk or pissed or asleep he is, Sean *always* answers his phone."

Elizabeth watches him, waiting for whatever conclusion he's jumping to.

"There was the name of a woman in Sean's phone…" August thinks aloud, verbalising his vague thoughts.

August thinks. He wasn't aware of Sean having a girl-friend, but there was a name on Sean's phone. Sean was leaving to see someone. A woman. They could be the last person to have seen him.

Carmen.

Was that her name?

"Why's that weird? Surely Sean would know–"

"Elizabeth, can you look something up on the computer for me."

August sighs. Bows his head. He can't believe what he's about to say.

"Look for local escorts and prostitutes by the name of Carmen. Generally deal with a high-class of clientele."

Elizabeth puts the name into the database and it takes less than a minute until three names come up.

"Do any of them have any other offences?"

Elizabeth checks through the first. Nothing. Then the second. Nothing. Then the third.

"Yes," she reluctantly confirms.

Carmen's picture appears on the screen. A cute freckled face, looking young and innocent, long auburn hair, daintily slim yet curvy body.

"Carmen Collins," Elizabeth reads. "Nothing for the last five years, but before that, arrested multiple times for assault. Received an ASBO as a teenager. Was arrested sixteen times for stalking but never charged – August, what does this woman have to do with Sean?"

"Just a hunch."

"Hey, check this out – the school we came across was her school as a child. She was permanently excluded for following a male teacher and attacking his girlfriend."

"Shit. Have we got an address?"

"Yes."

"Good, tell it to me in the car." He turns to the rest of the room. "We have an address people, let's go!"

Chapter Thirty-One

A GUN SITS IN SEAN'S LAP.

But he's fully restrained.

As is Victor.

This makes no sense.

He looks at the killer, walking toward him. They take down their hood. Step into the light. Their smile makes him melt.

Oh, God. No. It can't be.

But it is.

"Hi, Sean," sings the sweet, innocent smile of Carmen, waving her fingers at him in a sultry flick. "Welcome to my house."

Her hoody drops in a clump on the floor.

She wears a long, elegant, dark red ballgown that glides off her like wind down a mountain. Her hair has been curled; long, luscious locks painting her shoulders and circling her face. Her lips are decorated with a lipstick that matches her dress. She is lethally stunning.

"What are you doing?" cries Sean.

She walks to Victor and runs her hands through his hair, looking at him with eyes of utter detest.

"You said you couldn't catch him," she says in a low-pitched voice filled to the brim with abhorrence.

Victor does not take his eyes off Sean. The whole time he sits there gurning, lecherously leering, a sarcastically elated grin spreading across his peculiar face.

"You asked me this before," Carmen explains, "whether we could ever be together."

She fiddles with her lip and smiles in the way that would previously have filled Sean with a childish excitement but now fills him with a terrified dread.

"The answer is yes," she tells him. "Of course, we can, Sean. I've always loved you. There is no one else that comes close."

"What?"

She saunters over to him, her weight passing from leg to leg in a way that makes her succulent arse cheeks wiggle from side to side. She bends over him, stroking her hand down his cheek, looking into his eyes with the adoration he'd always craved from her.

"But you could never give yourself to me in the way that I wanted. Not entirely. You were so caught up in something else. You were so caught up… in *someone* else."

He glances at Victor's demented face that refuses to blink.

It all makes sense.

She glides to the ground, resting on her knees, her head level with Sean's crotch. She places a hand on each of his thighs and looks up at him, in the space between him and Victor, between him and the bastard he could never catch – but *she* could.

She looks him in the eyes. There's love and devotion in

there, with a fragility she's kept hidden. But it's tainted. Tainted by a delusion that she is doing the right thing.

Is she doing the right thing?

This is what I wanted, isn't it? Carmen to myself. A chance to kill Victor.

"So I practised. It took me five or six to get it right, but I practised. Victim versus villain. And I got it right. So I got it ready for you. Ready for this. So you can be free."

"You killed all of those other people for *practice?*"

Any remnants of sweetness about her float away with her flawless scent. In an instant, she is changed. Someone else. Something else.

But she doesn't see it. She nods like you would to a child who had lost their favourite toy and now it's being returned.

"I got very good at it. Problem is, the more I learnt about you and Victor" – she indicates Victor Crane with a hand, who nods as if he is being announced as a nominee for an award – "the more I got to wondering – are you really the victim?"

"What?"

Sean's eyes narrow into a piercing glare.

"Victor is doing what he loves! He's doing what he's wanted from day one. He isn't denying who he is. But you are."

"Who am I, Carmen?"

"A killer."

"I'm not a killer."

"You are. You're a killer, just like him."

"I am *nothing* like him."

She giggles to herself, like a teacher whose student just gave them a silly answer to a logical question.

"Sean, you are practically his twin."

Sean rocks from side to side, snarling, battering against his restraints.

"What are you going to do then? Going to give him the gun?"

She stands and dances around Sean.

"I will forgive all your sins, Sean. I will see you as the victim. Provided you do just one thing."

"What?" he barks, growing tired of incessant talking. Either he's going to die or Victor is, and he wants the whole ordeal to be over.

"Tell me you love me."

Is that it?

He tells her he loves her, shoots Victor Crane in the head, then takes her down?

It's a no-brainer.

"I love you," he tells her.

She picks up the gun. Holds it in between them.

Sean does not take his eyes off it.

There in her hand is all that's between him and Victor's death.

"Are you lying, Sean?"

He looks at her.

Is this a test?

Is he supposed to say he doesn't love her, to show he won't lie?

He sticks with his first instinct.

"No. I am not lying."

She smiles a smile that could light up the moon.

She drops the gun by Sean's feet. She walks to the opposite wall, still encased in shadow, and retracts something. Garden sheers. She uses them to slice through the rope wrapped around Sean's body and it falls to the floor like a dead snake.

She uses a key to unlock his handcuffs.

He flexes his arms.

Stretches them.

Aside from his feet, he's free.

He picks up the gun.

Victor Crane still leers at him.

Still smiles.

Still doesn't blink.

Still does everything he can to rattle Sean, to make him hate the world, to torment him, to taunt him, to make it seem like Victor is better in every way.

Victor. The man who took his family from him.

Sean points the gun at Victor's head and hovers his finger over the trigger.

Chapter Thirty-Two

Sirens wail full blast, prompting cars to part with urgency. Elizabeth grips the sides of her seats. Yes, she always drives fast with the blue lights on – but never this fast.

She doesn't understand why August is hurrying in the way he is.

She can't understand.

She only knows Sean now. She met him at the beginning of his downfall, as the Victor Crane case was introduced. She witnessed the rapid degradation of his morals, his sanity – hell, even his purpose. She has only seen his overly aggressive temper and his extreme alcoholic habits. She met the man who has sex with a whore to cure his solace.

But that's not who he is to August.

He knew Sean Mallon fifteen years ago when they were both constables starting out on the job, a few years before Sean's wife left him and he transferred to London.

Sean was a newlywed with a child on the way. His face fresh, his skin clear, his energy palpable. Complete dedication with such enthusiasm to the job. Any call that came through the radio, he would demand that they were the ones to respond. The adrenaline would give him such a high he was practically bouncing.

From there he became one of the greatest, most intuitive detectives he has ever known.

Yes, Elizabeth thinks less of Sean because she's witnessed his degradation – but August still thinks highly of the man he saw in his elevation to greatness.

Sean was so good with people.

Scrap that, he was great with people.

He could talk a killer into handing himself in. He could manipulate a suicidal man off a ledge. He could master an artistry of words that would provide a drugee with enough reason to rethink their life.

And how he loved his family. Devoted to his daughter, would do anything for her. Sheila, his wife, his school sweetheart. They were meant to be. It was perfect. Unbreakable.

When it ended, and Sean couldn't see his daughter every day, August saw what that did to him. But August also saw the buzz that would brighten Sean on his custardy day.

Work became Sean's way of life.

He was on a mission to rid the world of the worst.

When he caught his first serial killer he was put on a pedestal of the highest ebb. It wasn't just the police that praised him, or the press – it was the country. His name was mentioned in speeches by the monarchy, by the government. He was faultless. A shining light that blinded everyone with its magnificence.

But they knew the story, not the man.

August saw the scars that he saw. He saw what it did to Sean.

Then Sean took a man's life.

And he hid it.

Then…

No. August doesn't owe his loyalty to a drunken has-been

who verbally abuses his colleagues and spends his time stumbling over crime scenes and showing himself up.

August owes it to that great man. The one he saw rise. The one who fell captive to his own brilliance.

Elizabeth doesn't know that story.

Hell, most people who do are gone. Left for better things. Better places. Better jobs.

But August has not.

He could never have done this job if it weren't for Sean.

Sean supported August through troubles in his career, his marriage, his life. It was more than a friend could ask for. Without it, August would not have made it this far. He would be where Sean is now. The loser who stinks of whiskey, wears a grubby uniform and grows an addiction to the fake love of a prostitute.

But August is not the man Sean has become – and he has Sean to thank for that.

That is why he has to save Sean. Not just from his escort girlfriend – but from the hollow pit he has fallen into.

He skids the car around another corner, seeing the rest of the flashing blue lights disappear in his rear-view mirror. His eyes flicker over the speedometer as he veers down a housing estate at eighty miles-per-hour, searching for hazards, hoping that no one gets in the way.

As he approaches the address he slows down and turns the sirens off. He parks out of sight.

The house is dark.

There is no movement.

A feeling in August's gut tells him something terrible is happening.

Either they are already there, or it's already been done.

Chapter Thirty-Three

SEAN FLEXES HIS FINGERS. SECURES HIS GRIP ON THE GUN. Feels its rough edges.

He looks Victor in the eyes.

This is it. What he's been waiting for. For years. He's dreamt of this moment, he's imagined how it would feel.

He decides to savour it. Savour every piece of fear that flickers across that bastard's face.

He doesn't want to do it quickly.

He presses the gun against Victor's kneecap.

Victor still grins.

Sean can't bring himself to shoot. Not yet. He can't.

Instead, he pulls the gun backwards and smacks it hard into the roof of his knee.

Victor moans in pain. It's the first time that shit-eating grin fades, but it doesn't last long. After a second of respite, it's back again, and those awful eyes refill with irritating arrogance.

Carmen appears in his peripheral vision, standing behind Victor, waiting. She doesn't realise.

This isn't the beginning of them.

It's the end of me.

Finally, that poison in his desk drawer can dance down his throat with the grace of a ballroom dancer. It can fill him. End it.

No one will miss him.

Not really.

So he sits there. Watching Victor smile. Immobile. With no idea of the agony he is going to face. He is restrained. There is nothing he can do about it.

"I'm going to do to you what you did to my daughter," Sean tells him.

A bloody patch soaks through the knee of Victor's cream trousers. Those ridiculous cream trousers.

No, he's not going to do what Victor did to his daughter.

I'm going to do more.

He rips the duct tape from Victor's mouth and places the gun against his skull.

"Well?" Sean taunts him.

Victor says nothing. Doesn't falter. Even at his demise, he doesn't give in.

"What would you like me to do, my friend?" Victor asks. "Beg? Call you a nasty sod? What did you expect?"

That grin. It incenses Sean further.

"I can see it," Victor continues. "Even though I'm the one tied up, and you're the one with the gun, I'm still winning. You're still raging."

"Shut up."

"I am going to find your daughter."

"I said shut up."

"I am going to open her up."

"*Shut up!*"

"And lick the inside of her heart."

Sean retracts his arm and smacks the gun through

Victor's face. His nose audibly cracks and a splatter of blood decorates the floor, but his grin is still there.

It's always still there.

"I am going to watch her writhe in my hands," Victor continues.

Sean sticks the gun into Victor's mouth.

Points it upwards to make sure the bullet goes through his brain. It's very unlikely someone would survive a bullet, but Sean wouldn't even take a miniscule chance of survival.

"Hurry up," Carmen urges him.

The door punches open.

There August stands.

He stops immediately. Registers the scene before him.

"Do not enter the house," August speaks into his radio. "Repeat, no officers are to enter the house. Form a perimeter."

"What are you doing?" Sean asks.

"I don't want anyone to see what you might be about to do." August cautiously reaches out to Sean. "But I'm hoping that won't happen. I'm hoping you'll just put the gun down."

Sean looks to Victor's smug face.

To Carmen's expectant eyes.

To August's hopeful fear.

August. A man who really cares.

Because he knows that if that trigger is pulled, then that truly will be the end of Sean Mallon.

"I have to do it, August," Sean solemnly says.

August shakes his head.

"No, you don't. Please, Sean. For your own sake."

Chapter Thirty-Four

"Stay where you are," Sean instructs August.

"Okay, Sean, I won't come any further. It's just us."

"Stop it," Sean snaps. "Don't try police negotiation tactics on me. I know what you're doing. I've used them."

"No, you're right, Sean. Correct again."

"I said stop it!" Sean screams so hard his voice breaks. "You're using my name to make it personal. You're talking to me in a way to make me think I'm the one in control. Stop it, August, I know these bullshit tactics so don't bother!"

"Okay, Sean. That's fine. Tell you what, why don't we get everyone else out of here, yeah? So it's just us? If I radio a few officers to come and collect these two, would that be okay?"

"No."

August sighs. His hands are in the air. Sean can see the pain in his face, the conflict, the hope that Sean will do what August deems as the right thing.

What a silly notion.

Only a fool can believe in the concept of right and wrong.

There is no such thing.

There's just your decision or someone else's.

"I'm going to ask you, as calm as I can," August persists, his eyes tearful, "Please, put the gun down. Please, do not kill Victor Crane."

The one request Sean would never agree to.

"Get fucked, August."

"He deserves it, Sean, I get it. He does. But you don't."

"What?"

Is this another pathetic strategy?

It's ridiculous.

August thinks he can manipulate me?

No.

August is his oldest friend. The one person left he would want to attend his funeral. But in this case, he is wrong.

Victor Crane must die.

"Victor Crane deserves it – but you don't deserve the guilt that comes with it. Do you?"

"August, you–"

"You did it before, didn't you?"

Flashes of Alexander Shirlov's corpse imprint themselves on the forefront of Sean's mind. The blood on his hands. The blood that would never scrub away.

"Remember what it took for you to move on from that?" August continues. "Do you really want to do that again?"

"There will be no getting over it, August. After this, there is nothing else for me. I'm done."

"I don't believe that, Sean."

"You don't need to."

Sean looks at Victor. The gun lodged in his mouth. Any normal person would look humiliated, pathetic. But it looks like it's giving Victor a sick thrill. A sick thrill that only infuriates Sean further.

But August is right about one thing.

What haven't I killed him yet?

"Come on, Sean!" Carmen shouts at him with a crazy edge to her voice that he has never heard before. "Or we'll never be together!"

"Is that what you want, Sean?" August asks. "To be with her? Like this?"

"She has nothing to do with this," Sean answers.

"Good. Because if you're not going to shoot him for her, and you're not going to put the gun down for you, then please – do it for me."

He frowns.

A perplexing grimace wipes across his face.

What the hell has August got to do with any of this?

"Go to hell, August. This has nothing to do with you."

"It does, Sean. Because it's about you. Because I care."

"Piss off!"

No one cares about me.

Reduce it all down to its basicity and August is just some nagging boss he has.

His finger begins to squeeze the trigger.

"I know you see me as a useless superior now – but once, we were friends."

Sean glares at August. Is he really trying this?

"You helped me with my marriage. With my career. You helped me grow as a person."

Sean laughs out loud.

Helped him grow as a person?

Give me a break.

"I'm being serious, Sean. I wouldn't be standing here if it weren't for you. In fact, if it weren't for you I'd likely be the one sat in that seat holding that gun. At the end of my tether. About to do something really, really foolish."

Sean's hand shakes. For the first time since lifting the gun, the rigidity of his muscles falters.

"I'm sorry, Sean. I'm sorry I haven't supported you the way you did me. I know I haven't, otherwise, you wouldn't be here right now."

Sean's head drops.

His grip on the gun loosens.

"I should have done better."

"Stop it, August."

"But the truth is I was just one step away from having a breakdown and you…"

"Enough."

Sean decides he can't hear anymore.

He sits back.

Drops the gun.

August rushes to Sean's side and places a firm, reassuring hand on his shoulder. Looks him in the eyes and smiles. A friendly smile.

Sean smiles back.

"Thank you, Sean. Tha–"

Sean has no idea what happens next. It happens so quickly that he doesn't register it until it's all over.

Not until the gunshot has gone off.

Not until the ringing in his ears has taken him over.

Not until August's wide eyes are still in a way they weren't a moment ago.

August's body drops to Sean's feet.

Sean instinctively lifts the gun and points it in the direction of the bullet.

In the direction of Carmen, holding firmly onto her own colt .45.

Sean pulls the trigger.

Nothing fires.

The canon is empty. It was empty this whole time.

As Sean's hearing returns, he hears seven fatal words sing from Victor's mouth.

"I told you he wouldn't do it."

As Victor stands, his restraints fall off. He kisses Carmen on the cheek and turns to Sean, even smugger than when the gun was in his mouth.

Chapter Thirty-Five

MOONLIGHT IS SO MAGICAL.

The sun isn't there. There's no reason for it to be. And, even though Carmen knows that the light is the sun reflecting off the moon, she likes to pretend it isn't. That the moon does just fine on its own.

The bedsit stinks. As always.

His rotting body lays asleep in his bed.

They said he was a legend. Sean Mallon, 'the psychopath hunter.' All she sees is an overweight man with a thinning parting and ungroomed facial hair. His body odour seems to cling to him like a jealous girlfriend afraid to let him go. His skin is always greasy, making her hands feel like she's been holding bacon.

She's good though.

She makes him think he loves her.

And soon, she'll make him think that she loves him.

Nothing could be as untrue.

She looks to the streets below.

There he is. Her true love. Her true man.

He recruited her. Not for money, not for sex, but for her brilliant ability to be every man's fantasy.

He waves up at her.

She mouths at him through the window: "*I love you, Victor.*"

The man's a genius.

She can see why Sean's so obsessed with him.

Sean, so easily fooled. She thinks back to the café. Waiting in her car in the nearby housing estate. Watching as Sean approaches. Turning the engine on as she waits for Victor to depart from the café. To drive off into the sunset.

That's all it took. A different car and a different driver. And she could see the police officers looking helplessly in her rear-view mirror.

And the letters that she wrote on Victor's behalf. That she delivered. Ensuring that none of Victor's DNA ever touched them.

Psychopath hunter?

Legend?

Hah!

He wasn't even a man.

He was barely a boy.

And soon he would die.

And Victor would be free of him.

And the sunset will beckon them home once again.

Chapter Thirty-Six

CARMEN DRAPES HER ARMS OVER VICTOR, HOLDING THE GUN so haphazardly in her hand that Sean struggles to keep his gaze from it. If she doesn't murder him intentionally, she may well do it by accident.

They engage in a passionate kiss that wettens their lips, and the moisture glistens in the faint light as they turn to look at Sean.

"You're an idiot," Victor declares.

Sean doesn't move.

Carmen steps toward him. Smiling. The gun directed toward him, so stunning in her dress, looking like a perfect femme fatale from a 1940s film noir.

Sean doesn't say anything.

He just keeps his eyes on the weapon that killed August.

"I never loved you," she tells Sean. "You barely even loved me."

Sean doesn't answer.

He doesn't let his emotions get the best of him.

He can't.

He has to focus.

She takes another step toward him, enough that he can smell her again, the perfume that would tingle him with such anticipation.

"Victor has a brilliant mind. An unquestionable intelligence. You barely have a brain cell."

She steps forward again. She is within a step of Sean. She lifts the gun upwards, points it at his face.

He concentrates.

Can't think about his anger. His rage. His despair.

Can't think about his only friend left lying dead at his feet.

Can't think about the fact that the man who took his daughter's ability to walk is standing across from him, gloating, beaming with pride that another one of his plans has worked and Sean looks like a fool again.

"I begged and begged," she announces. "And he finally agreed to let me be the one who kills you."

She smiles her final smile.

Sean drops his gaze from the gun for a moment and focusses on her hip.

The scarred hip.

The one that would cause her immense pain should anyone touch it.

Slowly, he reaches his arm out. She notices.

"Aw, wanting one final hug?" she says.

She clicks the bullet into place.

"Goodb–"

Sean swings his fist into her hip. She screams with such intense agony that Sean almost feels the pain himself.

He doesn't waste any time in grabbing the gun and shooting her in the leg.

She falls to the floor, writhing, squirming like a worm, screaming, crying out.

She looks at the gun in Sean's hand.

"Kill me then!" she screams.

Sean looks at Victor.

Still smiling.

"I'm not going to kill you," Sean decides.

He picks the radio off August's body and calls for backup.

Within ten seconds, police officers flood the room.

Victor is restrained and taken away.

Carmen is handcuffed and escorted to the nearest hospital under police supervision.

The coroner arrives for August.

The Beginning

Chapter Thirty-Seven

THE FULL MOON SHINES BRIGHTLY THROUGH THE OPEN window.

The board has been cleared. The room has been emptied. Only one remnant of the Victor Crane investigation remains.

Sean Mallon.

He breathes in the fresh air floating from a narrow crack in the window. Turns to his desk. Opens the top drawer.

There they sit.

Drugs. Bleach. The two things that stand between him and nothing.

He takes them out. Places them on his desk. Watches them.

One couldn't be quite sure what he was watching them for. Sean had little expectation that they were going to jump off the desk and run away, as much as he didn't expect them to leap from the surface and force their way down his throat. They are dormant, where he had placed them, under his watchful, waiting eyes.

Just one big gulp away from ending it all.

It's what he's been waiting for.

He can almost taste the bleach. Already feel the lumps of the pills in his throat. Its thickness mixing with his saliva and swilling down his throat, choking him. He can already feel the reaction in his body, shutting down, pushing through his imminent, silent death.

There's no one else around. A few officers still lingering on the night shift, but everyone on both the redemption killings and Victor Crane investigation has been sent home. There's no one who would bother him, nor care about what he was doing. He wouldn't be discovered until morning. They'll be shocked at first, then realise that, in all honesty, they expected it. And it would be insignificant. Another mind too intelligent for its own good, destroying the loner who owns it, and alleviating the world of the burden.

They'll say it's a tragedy. They'll forget the arsehole he is now and rattle on about the hero he once was. They'll say it's sad. They'll say that police officers need more support to prevent this from happening again.

But it won't last long. Eventually, people move on with their lives. His memory will be left with a small box of his remaining possessions.

His daughter will be told nothing.

They will reassign his office to someone else. Make up stories about his ghost haunting it and turn his death into a superstitious joke.

His memories will be gone with the fleeting moment it takes to swallow that bleach and consume the pills.

He closes his eyes.

He sees August's face.

His dead face. Dead eyes.

He's seen a lot of dead bodies.

But none that had ever made a bit of difference to him.

None that ever thanked him before they died.

His eyes open.

He looks at the bleach. At the pills.

Picks them up.

Throws them at the bin.

They miss, but it's fine. He'll pick them up later.

He sighs.

Maybe it isn't so bad.

He stands, puts on his coat, and makes his way out of the office.

He goes home to bed.

Alone, but not lost.

Chapter Thirty-Eight

HE SITS AT THE TABLE. LUNCHTIME. ANOTHER PLATE OF edible shit.

Jack sits opposite.

"Hello, Victor," Jack says.

"Hello, Jack," is the reply.

"You're here."

"I am."

Victor grins back at Jack.

"Just as you said you'd be," Jack points out.

Victor smiles.

Indeed it is, Jack. Indeed it is.

Not long to go now.

THERE WILL BE A BOOK THREE

Visit www.rickwoodwriter.com for information.

Want to keep up with Rick Wood's releases?
Want two of his books for free?

Join his Reader's Group at **www.
rickwoodwriter.com/sign-up**

Also Available by Rick Wood

RICK WOOD

SHUTTER HOUSE

THIS BOOK IS FULL OF

BODIES

RICK WOOD

WHEN LIBERTY DIES

RICK WOOD

RICK WOOD

WOOD

CIA
ROSE
BOOK
ONE

AFTER THE DEVIL HAS WON

Printed in Great Britain
by Amazon

51638588R00113